Vultures of

a Kind

Kelechi Ezeigwe

Fisher King Publishing

For Tony and our clan. That this Country may
be healed eventually that our children be
removed from outer darkness.

Part 1

Part 1

I t doesn't matter if you're white, blue, green, yellow, purple or black.

You're first of all a human being and this should be enough.

We should be amazed at the unnecessary divisions and classes created by men simply to dominate and oppress others. I have observed how intentional these things are but how we are goaded and redirected to believe otherwise.

There's a tiny part of you that should create an awareness of the incredulity, amazement and often sadness we should feel in the face of what life has become in this world. The searching for answers in the face of chaos, the endless days of looking for meaning and happiness in this complex world, and sometimes for sunflowers that don't make it back home. It's like all the times you were at the seashore not knowing. Searching your soul and spirit for answers. Trying the embrace of nature for succour. Puzzled still. Not understanding the fullness of this life. The complexities of it. There's always that yearning in a man's soul that there could be much more and that one should be treated with dignity regardless of one's status in life.

There's the observation of aberrations, especially those meted out by leaders. We often assume that they should lead us properly and lead us well, but this is repeatedly not the case. It seems as if they have other agendas very different from their campaign promises. There seem to be other forces at work. Vermin of power. Very dark forces redirecting them to do very insidious things to the very people they were meant to serve, lead and protect. Is it not incredible how the simplest things in life become complex even when the simplicity of the answers stares us in the face? Why do we deny ourselves the truth and chase shadows when we could be free if we faced the truth and told the truth?

It's not the colour that separates, it's the lies often told in whispers, often told in unusual places, covered with white to look like they are innocent. It's not the dark blinds that hold the morning light at bay, it's the craftiness of the human will. The side eyes, the illusions that spring surprises. The spats often started as chats that are moulded in iron wills. Egos that take the thrill out of conversations of conviviality, out of the room, creating chaos that spills the blood. It is men that destroy good things. It is men that destroy countries. It is men that destroy lives. Let's be honest. Let's tell the truth! Behold the truth and be free from the clutches of darkness and the people that bestow darkness onto others.

I'm done looking the other way! I'm done shutting out the cries, the hollowness of our tattered existence. I'm done pretending that the streets are not flooded with hopelessness. That the stench that comes from the debris of rotten human existence, denied their dignity and littered on the streets, is not happening. I'm done muffling the cries of the pain of the passage of ignorance as a national anthem. I'm done beholding the attainment of stupidity and foolishness as a status. Here is the collective rape of a country, yet they say I'm a woman and so I should not have a voice. I should know my place and mind my language. This existence of ours no longer makes sense.

I'm no longer at ease. We are no longer at ease.

On the day that our young men were made impotent by their blind stealing of our collective wealth, their incongruous and clueless leadership, I was at a loss. Here I am, Ifedinma Obiakor, a woman. Just a woman… told to hold her irate tongue and keep quiet! I want to lift up my eyes but my entire being is solidified in darkness and my soul mired in silence of an atrocious nature. I'm dumbfounded at life and how it can play various roles; I'm dismayed at its upstart nature. I try to soak it all in, and yet, like the dance of death, it continues to encircle my head and take sleep away from my eyes. The nature of me and what I could become is malignant as well as benign. But let me tell you, it is further Siamese in nature. There seems to be no future in these places, but I clamp my mouth shut. My big mouth! How dare I say this? Who sent me to say this and what posture do I adopt in saying this?

Amadio, my friend, when you left these places, you ran like a toad being chased about by evil forces in the afternoon. You said to me, 'Ifedinma, I go to get the golden fleece.' Hahahahaha! I knew immediately when I got the phone call that you had run away. Indeed, no one who is sane waits around for the revelations of this country. The imaginations of hope have long been thrown out of the window. The resilience of a people crucified to tatters. But I come in peace. Our experimentation of living together is obtuse in nature, our experience of nationhood questionable. Has everything failed? Even the land upon which we stand feels different. Then the election happened!

We had hopes – for indeed, we'd had enough. No one went

to work on that day, Amadio. On the day they unleashed their power. The shrills of sadness could be heard abroad. Yet there was a heavy silence. We watched in exasperation as our lives went down the drain again. They said, 'don't talk, don't even sigh.' How in the world did we go out to vote and come back blood-soaked? The streets were empty because the jackals took over. The blood of the baboons and monkeys have been shed. Remember this prophecy of the blood of the baboon and monkey being shed? I'm sure you don't! So let me remind you.

It was a prophecy told to us by the one so thirsty for power. To him, power was his birth right, and to deny him that was to court death. The nation was set ablaze by his utterances. That year, the urchins of elections took over and there was bloodletting in every nook and cranny. Blood flowed! The blood of youth corps members handling elections was shed that year. They were young and full of hope. Hope for a better future. Hope eventually dashed and their bodies returned to their parents in caskets. We were bullied to relinquish power, or else! We were warned!

The streets were suddenly empty and silent. The goons took over the polls. I ran with my voter's card after I had retrieved it from under the table upturned by street boys after they took over the polling booth at my voting centre. I had left my house with high hopes. At the back of my mind, I thought this was a democracy and it was time to vote this nepotic government out. I was shocked at the length these politicians would go to just to retain power. Like fiends, their thugs took over the polling booths. They were fierce and ready to spill blood. They snatched ballot boxes and it was goodbye to anyone who dared to stop them. As I ran for my life from the mayhem that the election day had become, I promised myself that I would not be a number that day. We run to fight another day. The silence of our moans could be heard as they announced our collective imbecility as voters. So now, how will I tell you again and again that I don't know why you choose to call at a time like this? I am mourning!

The Bible talked about princes on foot whilst slaves are on horseback. My dear Amadio, our situation has become extreme. Even our neighbours are amazed at how we've become the teeth that grit and gnash the meat between the mouth. Our neighbours are bereaved on our behalf. They wonder at us and what we have become. Tell me, Amadio, when you pick up your phone to call home, do you say, 'oh, pick up!'? And when I hesitate to pick up your call, can't you hear my sarcasm? Can't you taste my fury when I snatch your call? I start with best regards and end with bullshit.

Amadio, the elders cannot sit forlornly again in their obi, the outer house where men hold court. They sold us for a kobo. I should have said pennies or loonie since the money you touch now is different. Amadio, now the things that were made for peace have taken flight, why do we mourn and hold dance parties at the same time? Does a father whose child was raped and battered hold catechism at the same time? How does he recount the tales of this evil to his friends? When his kinsmen call him, how does he answer? Does he answer like a bleating goat? Like mkpi, the he-goat on a tether?

Amadio, when you took flight, was it in the morning or the evening? How hot was the day? Why do you dream of news from the motherland when there's mud on our faces? How do we answer on the day that our farmlands were overtaken by herdsmen and bandits? Our women were raped, children burnt, our young men murdered. Can you hear the clinking and clanking of their cups as they drown in our blood? So they say that mockery is not enough; now it has to be dressed in a robe.

Amadio, the elders were in the house when the goat gave birth in tethers. They wore their red caps and held the ofo na ogu, the symbol of truth and justice, in their hands whilst their mouths spewed forth lies. So I asked, 'Where is the ogu?' On the day that ofo na ogu died, the symbol of truth, righteousness and decency, they came together and held a dance and had a feast on our graves. Our children were out in the fields demanding justice, asking for fairness and good governance. They said they had no right. What audacity! What effrontery! Tell me, Amadio, how else can I pacify you? When you see the toad running around in the afternoon, is it with clear eyes? Let me ask you again: how do you want to take a handshake then want to remove the elbow?

Amadio, you said you went to get the golden fleece, but I know you ran away. It's only an insane man that sees the madness that has overtaken our people and waits around, going door to door seeking out drinking partners.

How do you want me to answer when you ask if light has been restored? We live in darkness. We cry every day whilst their homes are insulated from the dark. An array of golden lights; their home. Our homes are citadels of darkness. There is no light, period! We seem not to be able to get it together, nor keep it together. I feel pain. Deep pain. But these people did not put themselves in power. We enabled them and accepted them and their ways, so they kept churning themselves out. Assumptions of angelic nature but distributors of deep darkness. Vessels of dissension. Enemies of progress.

The working of the mind of a people is always gradual, intentional and deliberate. The seeds of hatred and segregation are often deliberately sown and gradually take root. They used the weapon of ethnicity – which should have been a binding force of progress, power, peace and unity – as a force of separation, throwing us into war with each other. Our differences, which are a beautiful thing, were shrouded in darkness whilst they had their hands in the till and our eyes in utter blindfolds.

The eyes of the hyena are sharp; he can smell his prey from afar. When he plays with his prey, paws and kisses it with dewy eyes, it is foolishness for the prey and utter stupidity to think that this is love. The realisation comes only when he has become a meal. Completely vandalised and battered. This is the summation of our love story with our leaders.

How do we restore our sense? How do we make us think again? Even the ones born now may not have the wisdom. Our daughters, you ask, Amadio! I warn you again – when you call, make it brief.

Amadio, my friend. This is the tale of a country in distress; two women, two children and a journey of rediscovery and recovery of the self. So when I tell you that I am at a crossroads at what our nationhood has become, try and understand me. Again, when there is an outcry against our religious postulations, do not mind me. If I call out those that keep women in subjugated perpetuity, perhaps you may see reason with me. When I am bowed over at the escape of our youths from frivolous, painful experiences of leadership and rulership, perchance you will extend sympathy to me. Allow me the dignity of my outcry and my distended brooding over what we have become.

I am in mourning and the ashes of my pain and groaning spread over my entire being. My soul is in nomadic distress, my eyes sore with weeping. My pain does not abate, nor does my craving for peace and stability for my country. Your country. Our country. Stop. Is it bad to want good for your country? It is not impossible to hope for the best and work towards it. Is bad leadership peculiar to us? Why are we always in this place? This dark place. Without hope. Without a future. Always exposed to decibels and diatribes of lies and liars.

Eka went to church on a day that it rained and came back with shoulders slumped. The silence was eerie. She was only sixteen. A budding sapling. We could hear the whistling pines as the wind fluttered lightly on its branches. Even her mother – Mama Nda, as I loved to call her – could not wrestle it out of her.

She sat like one who mourned.

Eka stopped going to church. She was silent with roving eyes. Taciturn. Our righteous indignation did not elicit any response from her. We loved church and churching. It was a replacement for the bad leadership and the leaders bestowed on us. We'd go to church to mourn the death of the life we should have had. Even though we were alive, we could just as well have been dead. The prophets, apostles, prophetesses, daydreamers, apostates and crude men took over the pulpits and gave us new kinds of demons. Our lives became guinea pigs in the hands of mean fellows. Men found a way to complicate our lives through politics and religion for mere gain. We were a people bereft of knowledge who would not befriend wisdom. We gave these men the opportunity to have a field day. The more pain we felt from our government, the more the church and religion embalmed our pains and made them permanent. Now we suffer from hallucinations of peace. But we love it like that.

So all the times we spoke about the church, all the times we rushed there for ablution and to get sated from the wanton melancholy that assailed our depressed minds, Eka watched us with suspicion. Her silence was loud. We did not understand such emptiness. Some days, it felt like she was in a daze. Other days, it seemed like she was out of it. She went about her duties but stayed away from the house where prayers were often offered. At the mention of the pastor, whose draperies of purple and white robes summoned our sanctimonious minds to actions of piety, we always heard a hiss and a quiet diss.

We sat as usual in the open yard chattering, wondering at our plight, the hardness of our lives, questioning when it would cease, eating the bread of sorrow. I would often visit after work. Nda was my dear friend. Our houses were not far from each other. Then we heard a loud thud, then a shout.

"Mma Eka! Mma Eka! Quick, Eka fainted," Enu her neighbour called out. She was rushed to the hospital, our Eka.

The silence of the groove metamorphosised into awe as we listened in astonishment to the doctor's prognosis, but it was Nda's mumblings that made me wonder if I had heard the doctor right.

She turned and asked again, "Did you say she is pregnant?" There was a frown from the fellow and a little confusion, then an affirmation.

"Yes," he answered, "She is pregnant." And with that he left us, unceremoniously.

Slowly but surely, Nda turned to me. I saw the flashes of confusion, then the redness of the eyes, then the pain. She was in shock. This was her only child. A certain kind of succour. A shield. Eka was the child that made it possible for her mother to continue living. Nda in turn nurtured her with grace and some kind of delicateness. She protected her with all her strength. Eka was that child of consolation and Nda's life was firmly rooted in her, and now this! Nda wept so badly. No one could console her. It was not so much about the pregnancy. It was about her not knowing what had happened, when it had happened, and the silence of Eka in the face of it. Nda felt betrayed by her child.

"Why did she hide this away from me?" she asked.

They say that the strongest people cry the most often. The charade of strength sometimes often belies the delicateness of a soul, like a shield to protect the soft exterior. I heard her sigh.

"But how could it be? How could it be?" she questioned. "She's always in church. How can my child be pregnant under my nose without my knowledge? Who did this to me? She is only sixteen."

I put my hands on her shoulders and quietly steered her to a chair. She spread her hands and asked again, "Who did this to my child?" It was both a question and an outcry.

"Who took away my child's innocence and buried my honour? Who came into my compound to ridicule me? Who did this to me, Abasioo?" she called out desperately. "God, please help me! You keep me quiet? Who came to my household to snatch my life away, who had the audacity to trespass into my house like a thief, who is that person?" She turned and faced Eka, who was silent all the while. Gently, she took her hands and looked at her.

"Eka," she said quietly, "who?"

"Your pastor," she answered without much fuzz.

Her mother stared at her in disbelief and immediately let go of her hands as if they were hot. I could see the tears withheld. I could also see the determination in Eka's eyes. There was a certain nonchalance there and I could hear her accusations of her mother. There was total silence in the room. I was totally stunned but not overtly surprised. Such is life.

I heard the bell for the evening service and turned away. I was tired of our false piety in the face of religion. We had quite an argument in this regard, me and Nda. She stared at me with naked disapproval and judgment.

"God is good, you know?"

"Yes, I know," I said. "I'm not fighting God, I'm fighting the apostates. Look at us. We are here today because of their lies, their obsessive love for mammon. How do we reconcile the church and the society?" I thought and hissed.

"You need to be careful, Ifedinma, about what you think of men of God," she said.

"Nda, we are here for Eka, not me!" I reminded her. "I can't imagine why you are so besotted with them. Even with what has happened to Eka, you still cannot reason!" I was frustrated, angry and sad. She looked at me and shook her head.

How do I begin to tell my story, this impossible story that has become malignant and festering? Every day, I die a little. How do I wrap my mind around this contraption, this revulsion? How do I grovel in this pit of vomit? Who will tell my story, as e dey hot! Who will come to my aid? Why is it that these people have eyes yet are as blind as bats? What oath have they taken that has made them laugh in a pit filled with dead bodies, and to drink and be merry in a pit filled with maggots with pus coming out of their bodies and their souls convulsing with death strokes? What people, as others run to the light, instead embrace the darkness and grovel in delinquent shame? In the midst of shame they stand with pride, even as they continue to bow to the ones that put the chains on their ankles. They lay out red carpets for their captors and lay supine on mats filled with iniquity and filth, whilst they spread their legs to them and ask them to rape them again. 'Oh, how worthy of you to take me again and again because I'm sold out to you and I'm worthless,' they say to their captors.

At times when it's dark and they stand amid the ashes of

shame, pain, absolute want and stark-naked poverty that are fast becoming their bed rest, they blame the ones who often ask them, 'Why do you allow the rape? Why do you continue to live your life like this?' They laugh then, with soot-covered faces, shrivelled bottoms and mud-caked legs and arms filled with years of struggle, oppression and decadent captivity, stripped of their dignities without mercy, with roofs thatched with hunger and hopelessness. 'Oh, you don't know?' they ask, 'Can't you see the lovely chains around our necks and the shackles on our feet? It's a reminder of our everlasting yoke for the love of stupidity and a reminder of the years of the yoke of sweet love for suffering bestowed on us by these princes of evil and wickedness, our leaders.'

Amadio! Behold your people as I wait to welcome you home. Remember that these places have gone up in flames like the evening sacrifice, as the bush baby cries at night and the baby dies in the morning. Ours is a life sentenced to a perpetuity of lineage servitude and wickedness by the same people that promised us light but gave us darkness. Our own people. Our kith and kin.

Those who promised us bread but gave us stones.

I heard the bells ring again. It was time for the evening service but I was at a loss. As I gathered my scarf, I felt lost in translation: what is life, sef? As I rushed to hear the word of our Lord to be assuaged of my sorrow and cleansed of my sins, I wailed even more. I was just a wayfarer, a sojourner, but I had become a moron, an imbecile thrown out by a society that should have given me hope. I believed very early in the words of my Lord Jesus Christ, but here I was in the stark reality of the twist and turns of his words by the same people who should have protected them. I walked forlornly, even blindly, as my soul wept.

When I got to the pews, I thought, how do I present myself? How do I kneel in prayer? What absolutions will be enough for my rotten soul? Who will redeem me if not Jesus Christ? I was weak and weary. The bell sounded again. I thought about the man in purple robes that offered early morning sweetness to Eka and took away her innocence. The same man standing in the pews, he was the one that would say the grace and lift up the offering. I turned from the path and walked back to my house. Enough of this hypocrisy. Those that will worship God must worship Him in truth and in spirit. I heard the closing of the doors behind me, the putting on of the light. Enough of the hypocrisy, for truth should be told from the inside. I did not recognise this whitening of the sepulchre. I did not want to be involved in it.

I heard footsteps and I knew that I had a visitor. I peeped through the blinds and saw Nda coming; her face looked ashen, like the whole weight of the world was dumped on it. I really didn't want to see her. I was still in shock at her reactions to her daughter's situation, but I opened the door and welcomed her. She came in and sat on the floor.

"Eka is with the pastor," she said, her face pale. She sounded breathless. I took my time as I poured out water for her.

"Why did you take her there?" I asked, a moss of fierce anger gathering in my soul. My tongue quickly adopted an arsenic position, becoming serpentine, but I kept still. Be calm, I said to myself. Listen first, I cautioned. I grasped at the table and held onto it as I felt vomit rumble up from my stomach at the thought of what I was about to hear. But I listened.

Nda continued with her dark tale.

"If he can as much as touch my child, he should marry her then."

Hypocrisy! I thought to myself and handed the cup of water to her. She turned away from me with tears glistening in the corners of her eyes. She dropped the cup of water on the side table, spread her hands out and looked up.

"Tell me what to do, Ifedi. You always seem to know everything. You seem to have the answers to the problems of the whole world."

She adjusted her wrapper as she accused me of infractions I was not aware of, trying to get me to a place of sorry guilt, then blew her nose. I laughed silently. I understood her game. She knew me, she understood me, through years of friendship. She knew where I would stand.

"You think life is easy, but I'm here to tell you that this life is not easy at all," she cried, her eyes swollen and red. "'E no balance. This life is not balanced," she mumbled again.

I looked away from her and went to the kitchen. "Do you want to eat?" I asked softly.

"Keep your food," she snapped. "Eat?" she asked, "When my only child is with a man old enough to be her father?"

I thought she was mad, but I kept quiet. I struggled to keep my feelings in check. It was torture. The woman in front of me had lost her senses, I thought to myself. Religion has its after-effects sometimes, and it is madness and irrationality.

It has the ability to leave its practitioners disoriented and provide them with illusions.

"What did I gain, Ifedi? Tell me, where did I go wrong? Wetin I do? What did I do?" She began to cry. "What is the reason for my punishment?"

"Why did you take her back to that man? Why did you take her to the same man who destroyed her in the first place?" I asked with surprise in gentle tones that bellied my anger.

"It was a mistake, and remember that he is a man of God," she said lamely. "Don't judge," she added, looking at her feet. Defeated.

The fiery anger that rose up in me was like a volcano.

"Mistake!" I wailed, "Mma Eka, a man raped your child, your only child, and you call that a mistake? That evil man took away your child's innocence and you say it's a mistake?"

"Don't say that again about a man of God," she eyed me. My eyes slanted foxily and I looked at her, incensed.

"Man of God, indeed. How long has this been going on, Nda? How long have you been covering up for an evil man?" She looked at me sharply and in an alarming way but I was past caring. So I continued. "You took your child to a wolf and she was abused, raped and dismembered, and you call it a mistake?"

"Touch not my anointed and do my prophet no harm," she warned.

This is their mantra. Their national anthem. I nearly fell out of the chair. I had heard and I'd had enough! I rose from the chair and faced her squarely. This, my friend, this woman I've known for so long. This warrior woman had become weak in the face of religion and religious gibberish.

"Nda!" I almost screamed. "Go and get your child back. If you leave that child there, know that you're the one that raped and ruined her."

She got up without so much as a look at me, muttering, "I will not commit apostasy, I will not commit sin. The more I hear you speak against my man of God, the more I feel like my life has ended. I won't join you to sin."

"You won't join me to sin?" I screamed, "but you'll take your child back to the same man that ruined her?" She banged my door and left.

Who will bail me, who will assuage me? Where do I go? This is an evil cycle. We need to agree with ourselves that we have allowed ourselves to be used. We need to agree that our foundations are faulty. How did we allow foul men into our homes, over our heads and into our lives? Why do we pay obeisance to evil and dance to be hoodwinked? The lack of truth, the embellishment of evil, the kneeling in submission to collective wickedness. The banditry of hope. The idea that an insensitive set of people devoid of conscience can turn around one's destiny alone is a mad stench, a foul-smelling amnesia.

I call out religion today in my country. It has destroyed more people than it has healed. Instead of healing, it has brought us pain, confusion, chaos and the worship of mammon. Each man of God, prophet, apostle, seer, prophetess, is trying to outdo themselves. Merchandising the name of Jesus Christ to the highest bidder. It has destroyed homes, businesses, families and ultimately people's lives and our nation. These so-called men of God have become the backbone of our politicians.

I was once in a church where we were told to raise our voter's cards and the man of God told us to vote for a certain politician because God had told him he was the next president. He then released an eclectic barrage of curses on those who would do otherwise from the 'holy' pulpit in the house of God. I neither came out with my voter's card nor stood up when he asked that we stand and wave the voter's card for prayers to seal our votes. After that day, I distanced myself from the church and the pastor. Guess what? His prophecy did not come to pass. God is not a liar, and neither does He make lies.

People sit in their homes and watch the sunrise with their hands between their legs, grinding their teeth, groaning with chains wrapped around them. Metal chains of slavery ululating to the same leaders that kept them in the pit.

What do you call that?

So when I behold the numbness of us and the stripping away of that which makes us human each day, it's like a rock chained to my soul submerged in murky waters. We go to classrooms without ideas, hospitals without care, faced with doctors without tools and endless disenchanted hospital staff, given governance without hope, forced to live empty lives daily without the hindsight of eureka. The same spirit of mediocrity pervades all spaces, all institutions. Everywhere, there's the stench of hopelessness, poverty and absence. But when we get transported to other places where sanity is key, we sprout like olives and stand like oaks in strange lands and places. And our brilliance, craft and creativity shine like a million stars in other climes, with little or no effort.

Yet we live like slaves in our own country.

Amadio, why do we run from these places? Why do we fail to see the shadows behind us? The truth we refuse to tell comes knocking on our doors daily and bites us on our jiggered buttocks. We meet the stark reality of the truth on our streets, in our schools, in our hospitals, in all our institutions, and they say to us with the mirthless showing of their teeth, 'Daily you raped and goaded yourselves with lies.' We abhor the truth! To say the least. It's becoming so alien to us, even when we claim otherwise. Every day, the illusions of ourselves beckon, welcoming us to the deep darkness. 'There is a road that seems right to a man, but the end thereof is death,' Proverb 14 vs 12.

This is the street where we are right now. We are a stiff-necked people. Very peculiar in attitude and our representations of us. Often unchanging.

Our roads laugh at our foolishness whilst consuming the souls of our people, groaning with laughter as they consume both the blood of the innocents and the blood of those that signed the papers and their allies that okayed the projects. But most of the people that commissioned these white elephant projects are hardly found on the death traps called federal government roads. Rather, they fly exotic planes parked at exclusive hangars while they thumb their noses at us. You can run, Amadio, but don't forget your shadow's behind.

This is where we are. The bereavement of eternal mystification of a fraudulent leadership alongside men whose consciences have been seared with hot irons. Suckers of blood and eaters of human flesh, frustrators of human dreams, dignities and hope.

Amadio, we stand in strange places and try to nurture the hopes of the ones we left behind. Most times we escape from our truth and run to the sons of the mothers who took time to prepare the minds of their children to be wise and to take care of their futures by ensuring that mean, greedy men do not handle the leadership of their countries, only men of goodwill. The good book says, 'Train up a child in the way he should go and he'll never depart from it.' We wail that the wise children came and stole our wealth from us, deceived us in our ignorance and took our lives from us. We lament that after they have left us in our foolishness to help our lives, they still go through the back doors and make our lives sorry. This is a story for the gods. For how long are we going to continue to point foolish fingers? What's the stature and the measure of a man? Is it in what lies in between his thighs? Or his ability to take charge of his life and steer his ship and harness all the abilities God gave to him by making his brains work? I need answers, Amadio. A thief has brothers, even a prostitute. How do their relatives feel in the face of how they've chosen to live their lives? Shame? Or resignation to fate? Or both? To continue like a chameleon is to grope in darkness and endless shame.

I have come to realise that we have no shame. Please take it from me or leave it. We have no shame. We love to leave our history behind. Even our children have no stories of us to tell. And now our languages are becoming obsolete, even extinct. Our lands are becoming bare of strength because the youths are fleeing the land. Daily our strength is being stripped away. Our children are building their roots and futures in strange lands while our leaders and their cohorts make merry day and night. There is no one to question them. They owe us nothing.

Look, Amadio! Look at your masters. Look how their goblets are filled with wines of perversion, look how they sit at their tables and lie and lie. Look how fat they've become. They know that the children of the wise women have no hands in their debauchery. Even if they do, how long would we allow them? But they know we are not wise. They also know we abhor knowledge. They know we are greedy, that we lack accountability and love to fritter away resources. They know we can be bought for a mess of pottage. Yes, they know! They know we count ourselves as nothing. So often they wait around knowing that we can never, ever change.

The other day in traffic I saw Maso. Oh, he looked gaunt and wasted. I barely recognised him. I came close and hailed him through the wound-down glass and we shook hands. You see, with all the certificates he acquired from the university, he was in traffic selling gala. I asked after his people and he said they were ok. I sighed.

He looked at me and said, "Oh girl, you dey enjoy." Ha! See ya suit, executive banker!

I let out a guffaw and said to him, "Wait till you hear my story."

The traffic had started moving. I had to move. We waved each other goodbye and I left. I had tears in my eyes.

This country has the knack of ending one's life before it has even started. We love to acquire endless paper degrees, but it seems that the people who have held us imprisoned in our own country deliberately ruined our education system. To constantly keep us without hope, without a future. They educate us without promise, not worth even the cost of the papers such degrees are printed on. Our parents go through the gauntlet to see us through school, yet we graduate into an endless cesspit of a labour market that is filled with hopelessness. Able-bodied youths with serial degrees pounding the streets daily, only to return to whatever hole they crawled out of to eat the bread of sorrows. You either become a number or the number. I remember the rattling of the gang-masters and the ranting of people who did not know themselves. The meeting as usual was noisy with timbrels and exchanges of desperations and anxiety. A group of people who had hardly read any self-help books in years. People with no idea of what it means to manage others, to stand over them and talk to people as though they were beasts. A collection of hoaxes, a contraption of deceit. These establishments want the foreigners to believe that they are world-class in outlook and have world-class behaviours. If only they looked closer. They would find out that it's the breeding ground for oppression and a place for the elevation of mediocrity and suppression. Thoroughly capitalist, without soul.

It is a place where people are locked up in seemingly euphoric, pleasant environments whilst their lives pass them by. It is a place where bullying and bullies hold sway. This is a place where people use gutter language on people and call it a corporate environment. This is a place where the thought of coming to work causes depression, and when you complain of depression and fear they are surprised at you. These places are mad houses where they have their kangaroo courts and decide the fate of innocent people who are being oppressed, emotionally, psychologically and otherwise, by so-called managers that have no business being one. The 'marketers' were scourged daily. It gives me chills even now to recollect the conversations together with the marching orders. Even the memory of going for a meeting invokes ulcers in one's stomach. You have to prepare to numb yourself from senseless attacks at such meetings and stuff your ears. Even now, I shudder at the memory of it.

The chase for demand deposits is insane! So insane. You must remember to cradle and cuddle up to it like your entire existence depended on it! It has the ability to make or mar you. Your eyes, your entire focus, must be on the pursuit and acquiring of healthy demand deposits! Don't ask me to define healthy – that's your concern as a marketer in the bank.

Go and get the money! Give us the money! What about your father? Mother? Even your late grandparents take from the hands of dead people, mad people, any people! Just give us the money! Find a way to give us the money!

Then they bay, they belch, they choke on words that should not find their way into a corporate environment described as world-class, serving people with good technology. Some of these people have no business being here, let alone managing people.

No, Maso! I thought, I'm not enjoying it! This is not enjoyment. These places are dungeons of exploitation and meanness in varying degrees. These places cannot uphold the truth. They take away your youthful years and leave you paralysed in your winter years. You work like an elephant and eat debris. They promise you rain and give you dryness. They paint the picture of Nirvana and push you into decay. These are slave masters who take people's lives and dash their hopes. They mess with your sanity, your hope, your balance, grinding them to ashes. They leave you forlorn, tarn, tarnished, burnished, deformed and in despair. They have no regard for human dignity. These are foul places.

Amadio! One of their general managers asked me to shut up. He asked if I'm retarded since it seemed I had no grasp of simple instructions. I gasped. I only needed him to sign a document and there were knotty issues. I looked at this man perched on a swivelling chair and felt tears at the corners of my eyes. Never have I felt bile rise so quickly to my throat. You may not necessarily have to know everything or how to treat people, but you should learn the decency of civility at all times, especially in a workplace. I knew I had to leave his presence before I went ballistic. He was power-drunk and he grovelled in it. Countless times, I've seen him intimidate others to submission in order to feel 'superior' and in charge. These people behave like fiefs. These are not world-class in any dimension. They are contraptions of lies.

How do you contend with keeping a man on a level for five to ten years with no promotions when you promised at the point of recruitment that it would be between twelve and twenty-four months? What changed? Yet you keep declaring bogus profits all year round. How do you tell your family that the establishment that prides itself in trust being its hallmark is not trustworthy? How do these people get to the stage of taking people's lives and making them useless and a waste? Why do you promise rain and give dryness? These are contraptions of lies. Their beautiful edifices hide their snake-like nature. These are dangerous grounds; they take and take and take, then they bay for more. Bloodsuckers. They declare bogus profits, but you look at the people that work for them and they are wasted, wretched and tattered, whilst their masters hold goblets of gold blood to their tongues and in their hands, and bay for more, more! 'Don't be easy on those that don't give the result!' they belch. They dine in Paris today and wake up in Honolulu. What a waste!

Amadio, why do we blame the children of the wise woman when the jiggers in our sores are in our Shokoto? Literally, the answers you're searching for in far places are within you! They have you on a leash, waste your life and throw you off the cart when they feel you've outlived your usefulness.

Let me tell you about the collective silence. The silence of the mule, the looking the other way, the sabotage of the youth, the emancipation of evil, the filthy lucre placed on the table, the enticement of it and the betrayal of the truth. Let me tell you of the people that peep from the corner, tattle on others and betray the truth. Let me tell you how the truth gets silenced in corridors and how in bedrooms of filthy powers the decisions of other people's destinies are made and truncated.

This reminds me of the confluence of a certain kind of union. The union of strange bedfellows. A foundation of aberrations based on assumptions and misconceptions. The hope that a nation is here but has never fully materialised. In process, it was eternally stillbirth. In manifestations, it came with kwashiorkor. In character, it lacked candour. I continue to hope. We continue to wish that morning will come eventually. We are still waiting. Our hearts are still filled with hope. We rise with unmet expectations and dreams. We go to bed still unfulfilled. We love confusion and we love to walk incredibly in the disbelief of ourselves and what we have become.

How long is so long? Why are we so feeble? Why do we watch from our balconies the trampling of mercy, love, justice, hope and then turn around hypocritically and question what has happened to this country? Our country, our hope. Why do we think that we can cover the pregnancy that is obvious and tell certain stories to the strangers in our midst to cover our shame?

Why do you require accountability whilst you're ready to give none? Why are you so shameless in your hypocrisy? Why do we laugh in the face of evil and shame? Whilst in the dark of the night with slippery feet, we run amok with wicked ideas and exchange melancholy with the same people that held us in the dungeon of hopelessness.

Why do we laugh when we should wail? Why do we party when we should wear sack clothes daily? Who are these people in our corridors holding power, swaying with wine bottles, wine bibbers running over with iniquity? How did we get here? What is life? What do we leave for our children? What remembrance do we take to our graves? What inscriptions are on our tombs?

I used to dream so hard and place a bet that my country was the best place and no other, in spite of our challenges, peculiarities, diversities, ethnicities, the confluence of unusual and strange marriages that gave birth to ridiculous children. I still believe in my country. How did I come to such conclusions? And now, how do I wrap my head around these years, these fallow years of confusion and bad leadership? I heard the click on the other side, a long pause and a sigh, a heaving of the soul, complicated breathing and questions. Amadio, these things are difficult. They are complex, amoeba in composition. Yet you say, 'Don't give up!' Still, you ran away. What a hypocrite!

How do you birth a child that is an Ogbanje? Why the repeat birth? Why, Abiku? Why do you repeatedly birth these situations? Why do you welcome them to your homestead and run a warm bath for them? Why do you ask me these questions? How do I provide these answers to you? How long does it take a child to sit, crawl, stand and walk? How long does it take that same child to get to adulthood? How do you feel when you give birth to a child that has special needs and whose progression is slow, and you need to be patient and you are happy at every recorded milestone as the child blooms? How do you as a mother to a child born healthy see the child with challenges blossom and thrive while your healthy, recalcitrant child refuses adamantly to make progress?

Amadio, don't ask me these questions. I have no answers. Our condition has defied solutions. Our solutions have become a mockery to onlookers. 'Agadi nwanyi adiro aka-nka na-egwu o ma agba! Agadi nwanyi — adi aka-nka na egwu o ma-agba!' 'An old woman does not get tired in the face of a dance she has mastered,' she sang.

Let me tell you the story of a youth, a child of hope
– Chidumje. She turned, she twisted, she clapped, she
stamped her feet furiously. She ran to the approach of the
compound, a decent home. She turned around and she
shouted, 'Umudimmmm!' in a ferociously high-pitched voice.
'Hmmmm!' She breathed deeply like a gong. 'Unu anokwa
ya ee! Are you people around?' she asked. 'Kedu ebe unu
no! Where are you? Anam-aju unu! I'm asking you people.
Zanum! Answer me! Kedu unu. Where are you people?' She
blew her nose, her eyes fiery red. This woman with a head
full of white hair. Her exposed breast showed a woman that
had raised generations. The breast grew slight wings and
flapped to the right and left. She ran out to the approaches
of the compound again. Women rushed to hold her and they
struggled. Her voice vibrated with sorrow and tears fell from
her eyes like an open water tap. She wailed, 'Okwa nwam
muo! That's my child! Okwa nwam muo! That's my child!' She
cried, 'Umudimmmm! Kedu unu. Umudim. Where are you
people? Chi enwelu ehihie jie!' There was sudden darkness in
the midst of the afternoon. O jili eji. It was indeed a dark day.
She sang out her heart, this woman in her eighties – Ojienu,
that was her name. She wrestled with the women that held
her, then she laid out on the floor. She wailed and wailed as
the ambulance siren could be heard from a distance. There
was complete silence, as if on cue. Chidumje, the Corper
serving in the Northern part of the country and her grandson,
was back. He came back in a casket. The siren became louder,
then the wailing of the women rose up like dust in unison, like
a phoenix from the ashes of an ousted fire.

She wailed again, 'Chidumeje binie! Chidumje, get up.' She cried bitterly. 'You told me that when you come back, you will buy anything I want and you'll make me happy. Dumeje o buro kwa ihe a ka — anyi kpalu! Dumeje, this is not our agreement. O buro ihe a ka anyi kpalu. This is not our agreement, binie! Get up.' Chidumje was a victim of election violence, a victim of lies, a victim of a country that refuses to face the truth. A victim of a country that lives in lies and encourages the intercourse and impunity of destruction. A victim of a country that destroys its youth. Cut down in his prime, in service of a nation that has long turned deaf and blind to a people that have long become numb and used to being treated like filth. This is not about North, South, East or West. This is not about religion or the lack of it. It is about men's penchant to seize power and wield it. It's about certain men's romance with power being their birth right, even when they have nothing to offer. This is about greed and avarice, this is about a hijacking of the destinies of a people, especially the youth, by the few.

Today's men are so casual, so callous, indifferent, obsessed with power, its allure and allied forces. The kind of casualty and callousness that leads to death. I try to close my eyes to forget I'm in between, numb, dizzy and awake. I mutter to myself, 'Stay woke' — that's the street code in this country. I'm very woke. I think. Mindlessly woke. I swat at an unseen mosquito in the afternoon, my head full, my eyes closed, my heart heavy. I feel as though the darkness will suffocate me, conquer me. I cannot breathe.

Then from far away, I hear, 'Ire! Ire!' Adekunle Gold,

wafting out in this midday from God knows where. Ire, Ire, oni kin ma bo. I thought I was hallucinating. I'm drawn in by the lyrics and the melody. I'm dazed. 'The grass is greener on the other side, that's what I thought before I took the ride. I burned my bridges so I never look back,' he sings. I fight with what I'm hearing. A kind of soulful resistance. The message is profound. There is some truth even though it's bitter. I become weak at its appeal as I start to question some of my stance. Then I succumb to its allure, its melodious nature as it flirts with my soul, but not without a fight.

Our youths are leaving! Going! Going! Gone! Escaping the debris and tatters of bad leadership. Escaping the vice grip of hopelessness. Our mothers are waiting for their return. Some will make it back. Others will never be back. The world is experiencing our genius and ingenuity in various ways and degrees. That which was rejected has become the cornerstone. And so it is and so shall it always be that if you do not know how to preserve your things, others will help you keep them well. Some died hopeless deaths as they stretched to reach 'the good life' in other climes. They had lost hope in this country. Others arrived delirious but at least they made it. Some embraced the good life and never looked back. Some suffered hardships, shipwreck, slavery, harlotry, banditry, hunger – please keep this in mind. For some, their very existence has been wiped away, obliterated forever, never to be remembered. There is no recounting of them. No records. Yet their mothers, wives, lovers, fathers, siblings, keep scouring the horizon waiting day and night for their return.

I hear you, Kunle, I hear you. I hear you say that the grass is greener where you water the ground! Adekunle, what if the ground you want to water does not exist? What happens when the people we thought could hold the ground for us are the ones that are hurting us? I sigh again; with the sigh came the cry. I remember now, Amadio, my visit to Kokilu. I was told Kokilu was not at home when I got there. Amadio, you know how close we were. The last time we spoke, he sounded tired. He told me he had given up, with all the certificates and still no job. He told me he was processing his papers to travel abroad. The system had failed him. The job he had was not fetching enough to take care of his family. He was still living with his aged mother and his wife's work was also not bringing in much. I had promised to come and see him anytime I was in Benin. I made good the promise during my leave.

As I got into their compound, I saw Mama sitting under the mango tree with two of his children playing. Her face lit up when she saw me and she stretched out her hands in a warm embrace. Always loving, never judging. Oh, Mama! The secret of her goodness is in her good heart. This woman took care of us when we were at the university. It did not matter to her where you came from — North, West, South, East. It meant nothing to her. She took us in and cared for us like her own. Her home was a uniting front.

As usual, she went to prepare food for me.

"Ah, Mama, don't bother," I said.

She looked at me, frowning. "Nobody comes here without eating. You yourself know that. It is law and everybody that comes here must abide by it."

I nodded, smiling. I could see how weary she'd become

with age. After all the pleasantries, I asked of my friend Kokilu.

"Mama, what of Kokilu?" I asked. I saw the strange look in her eyes, I saw the sadness. She spread out her hands and looked up to the skies, and then she spoke slowly, very slowly.

"Only God knows." She spoke as if she was in pain. "He did not tell you?" She asked and looked at me in bewilderment. I shook my head in confusion. She spoke from a distant place. "It's been a year since he left for Italy. We have not heard from him."

It took a while before the news sank in. Then I remembered our conversations about his wanting to leave the country. How time flies. I wanted to surprise him. I didn't call him. I had been busy. Lost in the confusions of my job. I thought he would be home.

"Did he leave a number?" I asked.

She shook her head and said in a small voice, "We don't know if he got there. There is no number to reach him."

I was startled and I shivered a bit, tongue-tied. I thought about the horrid stories of the alternate roads and ways used by our people to go abroad. I shivered some more. The food I was eating turned to chaff in my mouth. She got up slowly and went inside the house. I could feel the unspoken pain and agony stiffened by age. I sat back on the chair and felt disoriented.

Here we are, now and here. These strange places. We left our homesteads, we fled our lands from the artilleries, the bloodshed, the hunger, the madness, the lies, the darkness from our fellow countrymen. We freed ourselves from unpleasantness. We ran for our lives. The grass looked greener with barbed fences, the waters were high and deep, but with wool we stopped our ears. We thought it was better to run and live another day. We got on these terrible waters for days without end. Nights without sleep, children left to the elements. Some drowned, some born at the turn of the tide. Our dignity was taken from us. We were no more than dogs.

The waves took most of us. We suffered in the hands of our slave masters who promised us rain but gave us wind. People that looked like us, spoke our tongues, gave us away and took us into slavery. Some days we held our hopelessness and tasted our deaths. We cried only in whimpers, no sounds. Points of no return. Willingly, we embraced slavery in our bid to escape our motherland broiled in incessant prodigious failures of leadership. Through the hot sands of hopelessness, we landed into scorching waters, wasted, torn, lost, forgotten, dead.

Amadio! I left Benin in despair, cracked, sad, insane. I lost my mind. I knew then that there might be no hope. Still, I wished that maybe out of the ashes of hopelessness a phoenix would rise.

Kokilu had gone to Italy without a trace. The mother and the entire family had not heard from him nor his handlers. I drove from that place bitter with tears cascading down my cheeks. Who did we offend, a land so blessed, hijacked by a merciless few? An evil kind of mesh covers the land. When our forefathers asked for independence, did they ever think about the burdens of leadership? That a group of villains will shamelessly ruin the land and pollute it is both unimaginable and unforgivable. There are no words to explain it, none at all.

Kokilu had run from the madness, and no one knew his

fate.

He ran from the confusion, the contraption, and now no one knew where he was. I prayed for his safety. I felt cold chills down my entire being. Kokilu was my dear friend. I felt my heart tighten. It felt as if I would black out from the pain. They say that the darkest night births the morning. We've waited for the morning to emerge ever since, yet it seems as if the darkness has grown bolder, with more tentacles, more ferocious, viler. Daily we sought the light, but the light seemed to run from us. Adekunle Gold, I ask again, what if the ground that we want to make green has refused to yield? What if the ground has refused our water and manure? Maybe people flee from our land because they have tried, and instead of the land yielding hope, it's yielded poverty, sickness, bloodshed and hopelessness by the day.

How do we explain these senseless flights to the unknown? How do we explain the deaths on these paths to saner societies where our brothers and sisters are enslaved again and plundered in this modern time?

Mama Kokilu told me that he said once he got to Italy he would call. She's been waiting for one year; no news, just silence. 'Silence,' she whispered. I grip the wheels. I'm lost, lost, Amadio. My own pain is like the rushing headache, the type that has your head in vice grips, pounding away. I'm totally confused and bereft of understanding. I dread the future. I can feel it on the streets, in the day and at night when the real owners bring the night hours to life at street corners, and I dread it. The emptiness is real. The hopelessness is palpable. I hear my phone ring and I wake from my reveries. My mother.

I pick up. 'You never come?' She asked in that tone! 'I dey come,' I reply. 'Come quick!' she said. Then silence. Since I took my leave, I went home to stay with her briefly, but my single life irks her. 'Why you never marry?' she'll often ask with wonderment and bewilderment in her eyes, in a way peculiar only to Nigerian mums in smattering pidgin English. 'Wait until old age, then you go know wetin dey. Shakara oshi. No husband! No pickin, I don see sey na dat kin life you want!' she'll hiss. To her, I wanted a selfish life of no husband and no children, and she was not having it. No matter how I explained it to her, she gave no room for 'the rubbish life' I chose to live. Then the ultimatum. 'Next time, you dey hear me so, no come here if man no follow you come! Get married before coming. I don talk my own finish.' Even with laughter threatening to burst from my mouth, I dared not laugh. This was a very serious issue.

I'm glued and gummed to a single life. My mother, on the other hand, cannot understand this disposition of mine to marriage for the life of her. Being single in this culture is not easy. The ridicule, the judgement, the unimaginable, the unexplainable. I'm glad she spoke pidgin; she grew up in Warri. If she had spoken in Igbo, it would have been deep and grave. Marriage is beautiful but not on the cards. Don't ask me for the reasons. There are none, just that I do not understand it yet and I rarely take on things I do not understand. My thoughts on it are rather strange. I'm rattled by its complexities and its winding nature. Never straight, not so clear. Never white nor black but imbued with so many grey areas. The unpredictability of it all. The changes. I will eventually but not now. Someday. Maybe.

This marriage issue is a story for another day, Amadio! I don't want to think about it nor talk about it. It's a story for another day.

As I drive on these lonely roads in silence, I ponder and ponder at us, Amadio. Whenever I remind you that you ran away, you always remind me that now you're alive and living. I know what that means. It's a reminder of the madness that has taken over our entire lives. The absolute dangerous and shameful looting by shameless men and women.

The lack of accountability of the organised and established looters who left their consciences in a pit.

I know what you mean, Amadio, when you say it is both deliberate and intentional, the chaos in our country. You said it was a strategy by the few to keep enriching themselves by impoverishing others. But I still do not understand the 'why', that is the puzzle for me.

So, Amadio, we may have to come to a place where I will have to ask you again; what is the 'why'? Why this mindless leadership? Why is it not enough yet, and when will it be enough? Why are they insatiable?

They created a gutter system and divided us by our ethnic groups, that which should bind us together. Our differences and diversity became our nemesis, our Achilles heel. They have become our defeat. They swallow and swallow like an eternal cesspit. The stealing is insane.

Six things the Lord hates and seven is an abomination unto him, according to the good book.

A proud look, a lying tongue, hands that shed innocent

blood, a heart that devises wicked plans, feet that are swift in running to evil, a false witness who speaks lies and one who sows discord among brethren. Proverbs 16 to 19 of the holy book, the Bible. We are specialists in all the aforementioned.

They have sown discord amongst brethren just so that we might continue senseless, foolish wars amongst ourselves whilst they continue to steal us blind. Their thievery is cast on marble and their evil goes to the high heavens, whilst we're thrown into the pit of poverty and extreme lack, stripped of our dignities, without hope, without a future, whilst our schools are run down, even non-existent.

Let me tell you about our schools, our public schools, the same ones that produced you and me. They are dead, so dead! Gone forever. There is no hope from the echoes that come from the hollows. No knowledge from the putridity of its stench, none at all.

They created ministries and parastatals and they've become conduit pipes of corruption. We are blessed with the best and the brightest in the world, but never can these ghoulish creatures create an enabling environment to harness our greatest minds.

I hear the click at your end. Did you drop your phone? Are you sobbing at your end? The things that I have seen have made my eyes blind. The things I have heard have left my ears empty. Now even my mouth produces no sound. I stand in awe at the magnitude of their ability to execute such a high level of evil and wickedness. Where did their souls go?

Did I tell you that Mma Nda left her child at the mercy of a goon all in the name of abracadabra? All in the name of religion, all in the name of mesmerisation, commercialising and merchandising of the gospel of Jesus Christ. The day I sent emissaries to her was the beginning of a part of me dying slowly. To think that a girl has no choice and no right is the beginning of certain death. And to know that all she can ever become lies in the laps of a certain man. To strip her of her identity has always been a cultural ideology, a worldwide movement. 'Don't speak until you're spoken to, reduce your gaze, lower your head, sit properly, prepare yourself for a man's house!' 'What does she need the education for?' they ask. 'Why is she going to school? Isn't that a waste of money and a waste of effort since she'll end up in a man's house anyway?' These are some of the prejudices, even now in the 21st century.

Then it goes on and on that even when she's run the gauntlet, had a good education, is assertive and as smart as a sharp, fiery iron, the workplace is still daunting, the political space still herculean, observing her with suspicion, making her work harder a million times more than her male counterparts. She's made to grope and grovel for a piece meal, even when she is more qualified a hundred times over. Even much more qualified for the corner office and the whole gourmet meal.

The day I called Nda out on her behaviour as regards to what had happened to Eka, her exchanges of 'see no evil, hear no evil' with the pastor, her man of God — the hypocrisy of it all — she slammed my doors and bid me goodbye. But you know my roots and hers go so deep. It is a song of memories of childhood and I can never forget how kind she's been to me.

When I arrived in Lagos at her invitation after my National service year, she welcomed me and took care of me until I found a job. Even now we live within reach of each other. When her husband left her, I gave her shoulder knowing she would do much more if I was in the same situation.

Yes, fortune smiles so differently in life, but real love when found remains a constant reminder of its endless possibilities. Mma Nda is that friend who will lovingly hold your hands through the pains and shocks of life. The first to celebrate your wins. The one that will stand with you through bad choices. The first to tell you the truth, however painful it may sound. 'Face your truth,' she'll say. Hahahaha. I laugh in bitter remembrance; how ironic. Now she is running from her own truth, running from her shadows. Such is life.

So I sent emissaries to get her to see reason with me. It is true that we seek God but I found him only one way: through Jesus Christ, my saviour. This remains my spiritual journey. Nda was instrumental to this beautiful discovery, and ever since, we've tried to find our paths through life differently. But then, like Berean Christians, I always search and search for the truth out of the holy book. I never want to be hoodwinked nor deceived by any man. I should own my belief and hold myself accountable for my belief in God. In the end, whatever outcomes I have in the afterlife, I will have no one to blame but myself. Spirituality and finding God should be a personal journey. No one should force their beliefs on you. To know that is to know peace.

As I journey spiritually, I hold the words of the Bible so dearly to my soul. It's been helpful in difficult times, depressed states, during periods of confusion. The wisdom it posits has brought serious healing to my soul. I've been enraptured by its contents and often times daydreamed of the world beyond, especially when people die. It becomes even more appealing because of the mysterious patterns of life.

I sought my friend; I wanted her to know that to wish away things and behave like they do not exist is to be dead whilst still alive. Confront your demons, even if it's a cliché. I want you to know that you don't hide your challenges in a cupboard. You don't hide away from confusion. You face them squarely. Neither do you tuck them away like a wisp of hair.

It's always good to find a reason to walk towards the light. A film of light is always better than a hoard of darkness.

I wanted my friend to know that she bequeathed her child to endless darkness, a life without hope. That a child suddenly got pregnant is not the end of the world. That our society will point at you with fingers of condemnation to failure does not mean that you're wrong or you have failed, and that they're right or better off. Life happens sometimes and it happens to us all. Accept this and move on.

Your adoption of hypocritical holiness and your references to self-righteousness do not mean that you're without sin and heaven-bound. We are all works in progress. I want to see your humility in the face of your greatness, not when you're standing in your shame. That you're standing in ablutions of piety does not make you pious.

Amadio! She sent word back to me. To ask me once again what was my business with the life of her child? Of what essence was my hard stance and why did I think that her giving her child to the 'holy man', who was kind enough to put a child in her daughter, was my business? She told me that her child was happy and that the pregnancy was progressing. She said I should shut up my lousy, messy mouth and mind my business.

Inside of me rose a kind of impossible vituperation of vile nature but I held myself and wept. I shook my head in sadness. You actually never fully know anyone. If I was told in my dreams that Nda would act like this, I would have fought the harbinger of such news. Religion is a mind game. Man is also a spiritual being welcome to the world's capital of religious manipulations, my country Nigeria. I'm heartbroken, period! Years of suffering has eroded our thinking faculty in the face of religion. It has become a form of elixir from deep wounds inflicted on the masses during years of poor leadership, and these wolves in sheep's skin capitalised on it to further impoverish the masses. Religion is part of the endemic challenges of my country. We ran to it for succour, but we became entangled and imprisoned by it. It became a never-ending pit of ridiculous and infinite destruction of lives and families instead of a bringer of salvation and peace. The more religious we became, the more corrupt the system.

The corruption is even more glaring in religious places. The shepherds became not shepherds of souls but extortionists, employing every method imaginable to extort broken people, sick people, hurt people, unstable people, even mad people, of the little they have. Their operations are sometimes mafia-like, mercenary in approach, wielding fear and punishment from their gods. This was where Nda had birthed her ship. No questions. Her pastor's words were law to her, yet he raped her child. Still, he must not be questioned. This is insane. I'm insane now. I cannot understand why the man is still roaming free, still dispensing holy communion and offers of ablution.

In all my years on this earth, I did not think I would be this broken. As I marvelled at the level of brokenness, anger welled up in me. I picked up my phone to tell Nda the way I felt. But the way I felt if I had spoken to her would have woken my ancestors from their reverie and their translation. I faced my madness, a certain kind of rage against the institutions of religiosity that have pauperised the mindset of a people and held them in bondage and obeisance. Tears were not enough for the searing pains I felt deep within my marrow, and I shed them uncontrollably as I sat down, slumped and stampeded in a corner. I threw an awesome pity party for myself even though I've never allowed myself to wallow in self-pity. Yet that day was different.

I needed to shed the tears and get my soul cleansed. Strange, how shedding tears is a form of soul cleansing and relief to me. I allowed myself to grovel in urgent desperation of relief. I loved that the tears seemed to wash away the darkness that held my soul. As I came up for air, sniffing, breathing, I could see again. I could wade through the cloak of darkness that wanted to consume me. I just needed to see the light, just a glimpse of it. I saw it and I broke free from all the desperation of confusion that had hit me and wanted to keep me bound. I broke free from its grasp, but most importantly, I felt free.

Amadio, life must go on in spite of all the cobwebs of the frills of our unquenchable urge as human beings for the immaterial. No matter how I felt, no matter how I asked Nda to look at what she'd done, again and again. If she's blind, she cannot see. For blindness is not only a physical attribute, it's often spiritual. If then your spiritual eyes are shut, the physical ones are useless, even though they're open.

Randomly, I tried to make sense of it all. There's a certain kind of pain that sears through one's soul in the face of impotency – just ask the man who wants to urinate but is battling gonorrhoea. How do you explain these things and to what can I attribute it?

My phone rang then: my mother. My life is such that I find joy in the wanton loneliness that has become me. I enjoy loneliness; that's how I hide away from the frills of life and the assemblage of camouflage of human beings in the face of the toughness of living. Sometimes I liken life to a cabbage with all its layers. When you peel off one layer, it reveals new and unexpected dimensions. Sometimes it comes all fresh, but some other times it displays rottenness and death within its inner chambers. Sometimes rough, dry and brown patches are shockingly discovered within its chambers even when its outer layers look new, and such is life sometimes.

My mother called again to remind me of the passage of time and the need to quicken my life by finding a man. In the totality of my Igbo-ness as a young lady, I've passed the age of the initiation into marriage and as such should make haste and get hitched. 'Of course,' I responded to her enquiries, 'I'm still waiting for a worthy man to come and sweep me off my feet.' The line went silent at the glum sound of my voice. I should bite my tongue. But I'm irritated. It seemed like sarcasm but it was not. For this God-ordained institution must be approached with sensibility and all wisdom before I end up in a mental farm. Messed up and done. It is culture, true culture, that when a girl comes up and grows into womanhood the real rite of passage are the marriage rites, no matter her achievements. Says who? Let me give you the answer: people, society and culture. But times have changed.

Women now want more, more than their mothers ever wanted, more than they can ever imagine. They seek certain kinds of partnerships where their interests are protected. Respect is primary and central. They also want to achieve higher goals other than answering as somebody's missus. Rearing and raising children. The spirit of the woman is elevated more than ever now! And her needs are very pricey. For she has seen the dilemma of her mother and the women before her and has decided to appeal to the benevolent spirit that a new path be formed and forged for her. She can't be on her knees all her life. She needs to rise up without needing society's permission every time she wants to rise up to her true stature. Without her intentions being questioned, arousing suspicions. The women of today are emerging, sprouting, and they've become strong believers that equal partnership can be achieved.

It is also with that belief that I wait to see this possibility come to fruition in my own life. But there's an Igbo adage that says, 'Ebe nwata na ebe akwa na-atu aka nne ya anoro ya, nna ya anolu ya.' Literal translation, 'Where a child is crying and pointing at, if the mother is not there, the father will be there.' So I understood my mother. There are so many conversations going on in our world today. So much to speak of, so many questions. Sometimes I hide away from it all to protect my soul and contain my mind and spirit. There's such temporality to life and yet we carry on like we are here forever. Things change, yet often times, we kick against the changing conversations of our society and we numb out the searching questions which we need to answer to provide solutions and clear away our dark brooding and questions. But we are afraid of our dark parts being discovered and our fraudulent natures exposed. We act like an ostrich. We not only live a lie, we embed our lives in lies and distort our history.

Amadio! The moment we accepted the general elevated evil perpetuated by our leaders, we changed our history, and our lives are no longer at ease. Our teeth are set on edge and our collective bottoms exposed on a grill. How do I explain these things to you? For the kind of lives we live under the governance of our own people are worse than slavery. We are short-changed, without explanations. The tears that fall daily are drilled out of my inner soul and my peace has taken flight because of the encounter of wicked leadership taking place every day. The wounds caused by doublespeak and the emergence of a hoard of robbers of the collective till by the same set of people leave me speechless. This brazenness of corruption emblazoned in daylight, the sorry sight of praise singers, whose tattered existence shows years of sabotage and stealing of their collective wealth, yet they still sing and dance for their captor whilst they continue to subvert and abort their future in plain sight. It leaves me insane! I'm so angry! There's a lump stuck up in my throat. I cannot swallow, nor can I exhale.

The slavery of a people has kept me awake in the middle of the night, deserted, lonely, in bed with my thoughts and the sounds of the night owl. Betrothed to wishful thinking. When I sleep, my eyes are half-open, glazed with tears. I am sorely troubled. Why do they keep guzzling and guzzling? Why do they keep swallowing and swallowing? What is this maze of darkness that surrounds us and denies us light and snuffs the life out of us? Why do we wake to hopelessness? Why do we wash our hands with spittle in the midst of plenty of water? Why are our certificates not worth the papers upon which they are written? Why do our children die in murky dark waters in search of the Promised Land? Why do our women take parched paths of droughty ground filled with land mines in search of milk and honey when we sit in abundance landlocked by a few? Why do we not ask questions? Why do we close our eyes and turn away whilst our children are killed and buried with denials daily?

These same cohorts ride on horseback and send their children to receive an enchanted education in foreign lands with our collective wealth. Meanwhile, our children take lessons in rundown classrooms with teachers who beg for their salaries and welfare. Why do they act like they're not part of us and thumb their noses, brazenly declaring us null and void? Why do they carry on like we are their servants and they are our masters when it is supposed to be us that asked them to serve us? How did they end up usurping our power and in turn rotated the baton amongst themselves, slapping their backs with loud laughter, clinking their goblets filled with our blood as wine is heard abroad? Amadio! The lizard that is on the wall and nods away its head in a hot afternoon when the drums of war are sounding is a foolish lizard. Wine bibbers have taken our lives away and all we do is to fill their cups with more wine whilst we spread our legs for them to continue to deposit their rottenness inside of us. Seeds of pervasion and putridity, the abortion of our collective future. When they're done, they use our tattered existence to mop the putrid discharge that soils our souls.

There are days when I wake up and I wish to be numb. My feet are heavy and they refuse to move. This is too much. It is too much, Amadio. I don't know how much time we have, for there's a long line of people not waiting for redemption, not wanting to redeem the Nation, but waiting to steal. The work that I do is coming to an end, for the toxicity and negativity of that space has begun to slowly kill me as a person. If I stay in that place, I may end up a certified nervous wreck, a wicked person, bereft of compassion and kindness, incapable of any display of human emotion. Unable to think, unable to behave like a human being. This place is shut out from the real world.

Or maybe I'm the problem? Maybe it embodies the real world, but I've refused to see it. The political correctness of it all, the pandering to subjugation, the belittling of another man and the silence in the face of darkness, but, ultimately, a gag order in the face of a vagrant display of arrogant, dark, transient powers. Powers meant to suppress and oppress you into certain obedience, the type that reduces your dignity and your right to hold your head high.

We're reminded daily of their capacity to take away our

daily bread and how fortunate we are to still have a job. So you have to submit to your 'superiors' because this is a privilege, not a right. Some superiors armed with twisted, fleeting, malignant powers often ask for favours of a decrepit type from their subordinates. Of course, when you dare to stand up against lies with the truth, be ready to pay the price. They paint a picture of this work being the end of the road for you and how awesome it is that you still have it.

Each time I go to work, it seems more complicated and gruesome every day. Like working in a dark chamber filled with robots. I can't stand it anymore for the life of me. There's the HR lady that asked me if I had a terminal disease because I was sick for a while and absent from work for some time. She laughed out loud whilst asking. This vision of hopelessness in front of me without empathy, lacking in kindness, uneducated in HR policies and procedures, enjoying a brief encomium of power bestowed on her for working in HR. Then I realised that my mouth was hanging open. Agape! She just made a joke of a situation that kept me in my bed for six months and had my family and me touring around hospitals seeking solutions whilst I battled holding down a job and being alive and keeping sane.

I needed to confirm what I had heard, so I asked her again, slowly, if I'd heard correctly. She repeated it: 'Do you have a terminal disease?' She let out a loud laugh again, a bellow of resounding laughter, and her colleague joined her. She tried to explain further, stating how ridiculous whatever ailed me would have been, suggesting that I might have been lying, even with my doctor's report from a provider used by the bank laying in front of her. I saw a nest of cruelty and callousness. I slanted my eyes, opened my mouth to answer and realised my throat was parched.

'Never mind,' I heard myself say. I got up, excused myself and walked away. So much for an HR interview on trauma and how to deal with it. It dawned on me then that I was in the wrong place. If a HR person can ask that sort of question without empathy, callously, without understanding that she could be up for litigation together with the organisation she represented, then there's no hope.

As I walked away, I told myself that it was about time to shift to new grounds, for to remain in these corridors was to court death. I knew then that if I left my destiny in the hands of these people after they must have marinated me, grilled me and laid me out to dry, I wouldn't be able to recognise myself. Uwa bu nke chukwu, according to Flavour, my brother from the east, the music genius. The world belongs to God and my destiny is mine and His alone to pursue. My journey. Sacred. This is my belief since I got to know myself better.

Amadio, life is a journey with different paths, different destinations, different arrival and exit dates. Choose your path and journey wisely. Embrace your God and trust Him fully. Lean not on your own understanding. In all your ways, acknowledge God and He shall direct your path! This is my core. My whole essence. My life in total summation. My journey.

I realised also that to leave my life in their hands, to even entrust them with a bit of me, was a channel to certain death.

And the likelihood of dying at the permission of another person, without my own ascertaining of it, was to order my murder and suicide at a breakneck speed. I needed to shut them out of my life and put an end to their power over me. To put my destiny in another man's hands was to die many times over. The outcome of my life is one I should own entirely. My mistakes should be mine to bear and should not be delegated. My pain, my fears and my beliefs should have my stamp of approval. The scars of my earthly journey, my badge of honour. I had to distance myself from darkness; this is my privilege and I had to do the honours. Anytime soon and I will be done with this arrogance.

Is capitalism without a soul? Or aptly put, is the soul of capitalism insensitive? I expect there are no answers. I hate labels. They have a way of taking essence out of truth and creating confusion where there should be none. Instead of clarity, they give you a jumble of ideologies, very complex and complicated in nature, that have a knack of hiding the truth. The world uses labels to hide the truth and we have mastered it. Unless you're observant, at first, you'll be enthralled by their proposition, but in practice you may become confused and shockingly surprised by what the labels eventually become – most times, hideously cunning in implementation. Labels are often used as weapons, their approach sometimes masked by vulnerability and helplessness. If you look deep, their makers and creators often use them to achieve selfish and divisive agendas. Their bedrock is often wrapped in confusion for the gullible and weak. Even the strongest and wisest of persons can get carried away by them. Is capitalism just a label? Is it insensitive, without a soul? No answers!

Henceforth, I needed to make my own decisions on my own terms and live with the consequences of my actions solely on my own moral footing. To wake up and go to work afraid of another human being will be the subjugation of my life. It was, to say the least, immoral towards me and my response was non-negotiable. It was not in the negotiation of this life called mine. I can never live in fear of another human being made by the same God, the creator of the universe. Whenever my time is done on earth, I wish to go out thé way I came. I will never live a life of oppression. It is worse than death. That a man ordinarily will stand in domination over me is an abomination. That I allowed him voluntarily is to question my ancestry and ask my forebears certain questions. Enough said.

You don't have to understand why I feel this way. You may not understand why it's so important that I feel this way, but please allow me to embrace my feelings. It's an abomination to dominate and enslave another. Even if you do not care. Even if you do not know. Even if you were taught to do so, nature did not make it this way. God did not make it this way. To be enlightened is to be humble and marvel at the level of wisdom and understanding at your disposal. But men easily use this as an opportunity to dominate and enslave others. Power is transient. Allow me the opportunity to say this and to wallow in the comfort it brings to my soul. So again, I say soulfully – power is transient!

It is strange to see men without mastery of themselves wielding power. It becomes a potent instrument of mass destruction instead of a cohesive vehicle for change and social good. It saddens me. We could be great individually and collectively if we did the right thing and actually loved our neighbours as ourselves. How hard is it? How cumbersome? When we are able to continuously and daily seek the good of others? How difficult it has become to see empathy, kindness, compassion et al in practice these days. The world is such a place. Enthralled with confusion, carelessness, selfishness, wickedness and the like on a daily basis. We are repeatedly introduced to strange things, strange places and strange living. You must be silent in the face of what is wrong, says the world. And you must learn how to say the correct, approved things even in your uncomfortable difficulties, embracing the lies when you could easily have said the truth.

So you squirm in your seat and put your chin up and lie whilst your heart is palpitating with accusations. You smile benevolently with the end of your selfish gains in mind prodding you on, asking you to align with the crowd and popular opinion. You want to be seen in a certain approved way. The product of 'herd mentality'. The 'look at us now', self-aggrandisement and self-preservation advocates. League of cowards. Complications of effervescent immaturity, lack of self-knowledge and belief in oneself. You are afraid of the 'cancel culture', the new fervent vocabulary in the dictionary bandied about these days! Used by the weak, the lame, the blind, the have and have nots. Used by everybody, and rightly so.

There is a time for everything, says Ecclesiastes from the good book, the Bible. Everyone is sore and stressed today. A little can make us tilt off the cliff. No solitude again anywhere in sight. Simplicity is gone, faith and faithfulness gone. What a world. You're not allowed your opinions in certain places without brutal forces descending on you. You are asked to be careful of speech and your verbosity of criticisms and suggestions because of its ability to maim you and take away your total freedom. You may also disappear because of speech. These are strange and uncertain times in my country.

In tears, I climbed the steps to sit at meetings that did not add anything to my life any longer. I had overstayed my welcome. The meetings were filled with chaff and at times lots of empty bantering that proffered no solutions. I was mortified to hear a manager pledge allegiance of his children to the service of this organisation because the owner promised to sack them since they were tired, old and ineffective, and to employ their own children in their place. He stood up grinning from ear to ear, elated and happy for the future of his children. I sat at my corner observing, cringing at this display of novice and naivety.

Then it hit me – not everyone will see the light. Some will see it and not recognise it, whilst others will see it, recognise it and not walk towards it. Some minds are shut down. It will need a lot of relearning and unlearning for them to see differently and hope differently. Some just never will, I realise. This is all they want, and I have no right to judge nor wish differently for them, even though I earnestly wish that their eyes would be opened. But they do not want to be dislodged from their temporal satisfaction of peace and comfort. How dare I remind them how temporal their bliss is and how odious their situation? Some will win in this game of life. Some will never win, no matter how the game is played. This is just the plain and simple truth.

You make enemies when you see the light and introduce it to blind people because it makes them uncomfortable. It has the ability to demand actions from them and they don't want this. They are comfortable in their remission; they would not want you to remind them of what could possibly be and put them in distress. So they embrace this type of blindness and envelope themselves in it because it's easy, it is blissful ignorance and demands no hard work nor hard thinking from them. You need some knowledge to discover and share according to the understanding of a few, otherwise you make strong enemies of those averse to light. You make strong enemies of those who do not think the way you do, see the way you see, nor believe the way you do. The world is such a place.

The light you see may mean and portend darkness for another. The path you take may seem like death to another. The truth you tell may mean lies to another. The world is such a place. You need to recognise this, accept this and respect the boundaries. Therefore, in moving forward with your convictions, you need not explain, you need not wait for validation; just take a rain check. If your soul says yes, don't look at naysayers. Remember, they will always be there at every point in your life. The Nichodemuses, the Pontius Pilates, Herods, Herodiases and the Judases: they will always be around. If you can, enjoy the ride with them, but recognise when it's time to throw them off your cart.

The burdens of decisions are carried around every day

since decisions are made daily and are so hard sometimes because you have to face the truth and the possibility of failure or wrong choices. I have come to believe that certain decision-making is for the brave and the courageous. Some can take a while, then emerge slowly, while still perfecting the choice and the shape it will be made in.

There are days, Amadio, when all I do is wonder at life and wonder at the chameleon-like attitude of human beings. Sometimes when you call, I'm bereft of how to pick up and the answers to provide to you.

Why do you ask and why are you bothered? Hahaha, I laugh. Is it for the love of the fatherland? You have made it to safety and your children are safe now. Their future is secured. You've taken them away from violent leadership and wanton cravings. Your gravy is cooked and broiled. You've achieved the dream of some of our countrymen, the dream of some Nigerian youths.

The day you told me you finally moved them to join you, I sat in a corner in my room and rejoiced for you. My friend, I can no longer lie to myself that there is a realistic end to this madness. It seems as if when we think we've seen it all, it shows itself like a peacock in varying arrays of blinding colours. Strutting mindlessly before our gnarled hands and feet, taunting us to do our worst. They need not taunt us, for what they see are dead men walking. We gave up hope a long time ago.

Our impotence as a people is well known, well documented amongst the good children of good women that ensured that they did the right things in the country of the people that got it right. The same place where you ran to because of the ineffectual leadership of our country, your country, my country, their country, our great country. The same place which has become the dream of every youth of our great nation. The same place which through hellish, ghoulish waters and unnecessary paths, our youths have been consumed and destroyed in their quest for better lives.

We have become a laughingstock, our children and youths hailed as thieves. In turn, they have branded our youths as lazy after stealing their collective wealth. They have set examples of the gutter type and have refused to be accountable as year after year they hand down desolation and depression and hopelessness to the populace. They eat and wipe their soiled hands on the collective fabric of the common man whilst they stomp on him at will. We move now as if we are in blindfolds. Some of us wishing, waiting, praying for the morning to come, believing in a hope they keep dashing. How long is too long, Amadio? Are we forever in recess as a country, or are we on a pause? Don't answer!

It's been a long time, Amadio, since I heard from Nda – Mma Eka, like you love to call her – but yesterday she called and asked that I come and see her, and I agreed.

It's been long that we spoke. I'm still angry and mortified at the evil she exposed her child to and the brazenness of this act, the dumping of her only child at the feet of her perpetrator, the justification of it all in her sight, the despicable way she shunned my chagrin. She poured scorn on my chagrin and swept it under her feet. I used to think that religion should bring awareness to one's soul and that as one seeks redemption and a higher spirituality, one should not leave their brain behind.

There seems to be a correlation between religion and the emasculation and subjugation of our people. It seems that after taking the beatings from the politicians, religion and the churches provide our people with some sort of illusions and delusions of abstract quality. It makes me wonder if we ever make haste to acquire knowledge and understanding to help our lives. Instead, it seems we open our minds, our souls and our lives to acquire confusion and wind. It seems that when it comes to religion and its conduits, we leave deep reflections and deep questioning at home. It seems we love to grovel in abject foolishness to the height of moronic proportions. We often never question these people in religious garbs, nor do we think through their postulations.

In a country where there are so many churches, with a people that lean towards the supreme God and believes in the Almighty, we are still the corruption and poverty capital of the world. The irony is that this is a country with massive wealth and massive human capital with raw talents. The more churches we have, the more corrupt we have become. The more wicked our leaders. The messages on their pulpits are not of transformation from bad to good, nor about the redemptive power of Jesus Christ. The name of Jesus Christ is their merchandising tool. The minds of the people, their playground; they are masters of deceptions, masters in doublespeak. The messages on their pulpits are about how to believe and acquire wealth without hard work. Their front rows are filled with thieving politicians who come back to bless their churches with stolen communal wealth.

We often do not read the good book to get intimate with the word of God and they know this. We then open ourselves to the twists and turns, the translations and vain imaginations of mean men, who only seek to hold us in bondage and milk us for the benefit of their twisted souls and minds until they replace God and erect themselves in His place. There is no difference between these citadels of deception, these gulags of corruption, and the politicians that rule our existence with dishonesty daily. I believe the Bible in its entirety and will often avail myself of reading its holy contents to safeguard myself from wolves in sheep's clothing. Our country is rife with a religiosity that does not show up in our value systems, nor in the attitude and actions of our people.

Amadio, this is a story for another day, though I suspect you know this more than me. It seems to me that you're unusually silent today. Never mind. I'm in a ranting mood and I believe I have your ear. I can feel your lethargic coldness even as I speak with you. My brother, this life 'na pot of beans'. We have to find a way to continue living without losing our minds. Life is tough, twisted and complex. Our country is cold and revolting.

I went to see Nda and what I met shrivelled me, disarmed me and reduced me. Life is a never-ending song with variations and versions but there are some kinds of music that one should not give oneself to. Don't ever dance to egwu muo, the spirit and masquerade dance. It is not for the uninitiated. It is a song from the dead of night when the spirits come out of their holes into the world to trade and hobnob with mere men. Only the initiated hear and dance to it. Do not welcome its drumbeats. Do not nod to its sound when you hear it. It has death in its pouch, but I digress. Out of the corners of my eyes, I saw a shadow lying down on a chair. I also saw the protruding stomach of someone that looked like withered pumpkin leaves, a shadow. Then I recognised her.

"Eka!" I whispered in shock. Her mother sat near her, shaking her head whilst motioning me to sit down.

Still, I stood, trying to find my balance, not knowing what to say, and I whispered again as if in a trance: "Eka!" Then I walked towards the shadow.

Just then, she stirred and made to get up. I stood transfixed. Her mother held her, adjusting the pillows around her. She coughed a mirthless cough and spat out dry sputum. I was still transfixed as I realised I was shaking, and tears ran down my eyes.

"What happened?" I managed to find my voice.

Nda, Mma Eka, spoke first. "Sit down, you've been standing since you came."

My legs were heavy as if they were fitted with iron. My mind was cathartic. I walked towards a chair and sat down.

It's not a right or wrong answer. I'm not expecting you to tell me the truth. When I whimper, I remember that all your life you've never, ever faced the truth. Let me tell you about two-faced people: they hide the truth in the darkness whilst they present a lie in the light. Let me tell you how people speak from the two sides of their mouths. They blink their eyes and roll them whilst they open their mouths and release a white foam of lies. I'm done with having my hands between my legs. Now I spread them and place them on my hips and face the liars. You should do the same when faced with them.

Once, I told the truth in some places where they said it was sacred, but I was able to discern that there is never going to be anything sacred in a place where truth is constantly crucified and buried. But I was not afraid as I challenged the lie. I became an outsider, an outcast and an anathema, but I was freed from bondage. With the spoken truth out in the open, I could own myself. There was no need to hide nor apologise for this life of mine. But little did I know that truth is not free; it comes fitted with a price, an ironclad price, which was my choice and mine alone to pay. I had no privilege to, I told you so! A pound of flesh nor validation, for I had since moved on, but I did not forget the after-taste nor the trails of their bitter residue. I still have the memory and the after-taste of my disgust of them and their bitter residue framed and forgotten in the gutter.

How long? So long, that's what I should say, for once a people have believed lies about their very own existence and conjured and stamped their death, there will never be a resurrection. It will be too hard to achieve. Here we are, a people bedevilled by evil worshippers of vipers in government, the mass production of blind men and women clapping and dancing as their lives and futures are stolen from them every day. But I think the leaves are turning from brown to green; they are sprouting. Dusk is coming but there seems to be an entrance of light. Yet it seems that there is a generation that will say, 'No!' They are emerging slowly, bearing light. Very stubborn in their ways. Ready to run the gauntlet.

I think they're in the cracks in the walls — forming, binding, cementing. Very, very soon, one step at a time, they will emerge. I hear their catcalls, very determined. They are coming! As you continue to sway to their music, take heed, for they are coming with demands of truth in their pouches. These vipers are never satisfied. No matter how you cry about your leprous legs, your sore buttocks, they do not care. They have you, your future and the future of your children, in vice grips of destruction.

They know you're a dead man walking. That's why they keep recycling themselves to the ruins of you.

The day that truth died, they erected a nation, yoked it together and gave it a name that did not belong to it. That's the danger in accepting strange names. You never fully become it, never fully understand nor embody it. Once you wear a strange name, you begin to act strangely; even when the name is announced, you may not recognise it as yours and so will not answer. It brings complications and certain death because you will always grapple with your identity, and you will never fully recover from the confusions that come with a name that is not yours. Aliens and strangers will often capitalise on this to keep you in perpetual confusion and in so doing deceive you into relinquishing your humanity, your rights, your languages, your culture. It's better to be dead and gone than to bear a false name.

To take you away from your ancestral rights is to break the bonds between you and animuo, the spirit world where your whole essence lays, your journey carburetted, your mileage stored and accounted for. Therefore, whatever happens, refuse a false name, reject it and solemnly mourn it. Do not allow it. To do so is to keep yourself in capsules of bondage. Amadio, is our name our trouble? If you know, please tell me. Often, you keep your lips sealed and behave like you cannot talk.

They made a wreath from the graveside and decorated it, gave it a name. On its head, they stamped the approval of hopelessness, deceit and foolery and it set sail. It became a country strangely, without an agreement from all the entities, without a character. Today, it has diarrhoea and is often sick because of the strange name that yokes it together.

We've often wondered from afar what gave rise to this type of malaise that has defied all cures. Nobody can cry for you, yes; nobody can wail for you when you're dead and your rump is decayed and you're still walking up and down in your misery, and you refuse to be buried so that you may have a chance at rebirth. No one can cry for you. In fact, the heavens reject you; even the earth upon which you stand denies you. I've never seen a man that is drowning and yet does nothing to save himself. Even clutching at a straw would be deemed wise. What a people! As they are swallowed up, they clap and dance and yearn for more oppression from those that held them bound. But the storm is gathering! They're coming. The day is here! Anytime soon! These new sets of children! The wind has blown and we've seen the chicken's rump.

We know what you do in darkness; it's being revealed in the light. Judgment day is coming and it won't be long. The blood of the innocent that you snuffed out is crying and baying for justice. It won't be long, I tell you! It won't be long and the birds will come home to roost.

I wake from my deep thoughts and translations as I stare at Mma Eka. What madness has overtaken you that this child entrusted into your hand by Chukwu, the big God, should be allowed to suffer because of your belligerent love for the allure of religion and its attendant madness? Is it the clapping that assuages you? Or the swaying to the cymbals that becomes you? Which is it? In my confusion, I die many times. For how can I allow another man while I'm alive to place the yoke of illusions on me and take my mind away? How can I allow my mind to be seared by the hotness of another man's dominion and bewitchment, and bestow on me the burdens and patterns of life, the one my God has not made for me nor intended for me? What is it, that he can proclaim over me which I cannot receive directly from God?

In a moment of my being downgraded because of my gender and being handed down obstructions and limitations not by my maker but by society, by fellow men, I will never allow myself to go down without a fight. I will always do my best regardless and take up the mantle of life and run daily. My womanhood should not be a reduction; it should be an elevation, something of pride, worthy of celebration and appreciation. That men, societies and certain communities have often approached it with suspicion and treated it with ridicule does not mean that they are right.

From a faraway land, I heard my name. Oh, my life — I will never allow a name that is not mine to be given to me, neither will I allow ablutions in such name nor be baptised in it. What is in a name? I ask again: what is in a name? A name is an ancestral burden. It is a map, a road finder. It is a light, a beacon of hope. It can become a breach or a stalemate. So, often times, I stand against bastard names, a name acquired carelessly, a name acquired out of prostitution on a drunken night or through banditry or a night of debauchery or brawl. I felt hands on my knees but there were tears in the corners of my eyes. I just wanted to scream at the unfairness of it all.

Man's inhumanity to man is shrouded in all foolishness, evil and esoteric wickedness. 'In the spirit, I rose and I stood on the threshold and saw afar, across many waters.' I saw what could have been but never was because man will always be his own worst enemy. When a man dies and lies in state, it reminds you that this is just a journey and no one will be here forever. Why then do we act the way we act like it all ends here?

I heard her cough, harsh and brittle, then there was the roughness of breathing and I felt pain sear through my soul. That my friend had allowed this upon her child, without thoughts of mercy led on by religious hallucinations, sucked the life out of me.

I felt her hands again on my knees then she spoke to me, but it was a distant sound of shame and misery.

"You've sat for a long time like this without talking, eh, Ifedi," she said gently. "There's no need to cry. She's still alive," she said subtly. It was then I turned and faced her, but my voice was just in whispers. A crackly, whisper-like voice, without volume nor depth. Deep, desperate and asking for explanations.

"Nda!" I whispered, "Did you just say she is still alive? So you wanted her dead? What manner of woman are you?

Are you so wicked that you can sell your child into slavery?" She tried to cover my mouth!

"Shh," she whispered. Then I saw the tears in her eyes and the way she pleaded with them. Then I softened. "Please," she said again and clamped her hands together. "I beg you, Ifedi biko. Ifedi, please bear with me in my moment of sorrow and pain, biko. Please!" Speaking trappings of Igbo she had learnt from association.

"Nda," I sobbed, "this is not right. Why would you choose this path? Why? Why are you so blind? Why would you let your child be sacrificed on the altars of a gigolo-like religion with the ultimate defrauding of a people to stand with them in the place where men lie against God – why? Why would you be hoodwinked by their theatrics? Why, Nda? I just cannot understand this! This is too much for me!"

Tears ran freely from my eyes and we held onto each other and sobbed. We sobbed because we knew the truth but refused to tell it and live in it as a people and as a country. We refused to be accountable in the face of failure and shame. We are a country and people in denial, extremely obtuse in disposition.

I've refused to be anything but myself. I've refused strange names and strange embargoes placed on my existence by a dark society and by people who want me to shut up and disappear. Nobody plays any song for me with lyrics not provided and approved by me, for me. Your assumptions of me belong to you and your imagination alone. Your judgments are not a deterrent to the way I have chosen to live my life. How dare I relinquish my power to live, into the hands of mean, careless men, when I know that life is fragile?

Destruction is always a threat; quick and never far off. Be mindful of this if you're meek, simple and full of naivety. Even more so if you're powerful and full of authority. I say it again: destruction is never far away. Be very wary if you have a lot of money to waste on worldly pleasures. Life is a race. Set your own pace very objectively and do the work needed. Who cares about their judgements and their approvals? I come the way I am, my warts and all. Stop waiting for it, their validations, their approvals, I told myself aeons ago; take the road less travelled and it will save you. Make sure to travel light. Drop your baggage and be free. Be bold, be you.

Seek not their permission, and by this I mean the people of the world. Those who wait by the balconies of life as umpires, as critics, with tape rulers measuring other people's races and accomplishments with no thought to their own. Be thankful to them for this gift; they help make life interesting. I cannot imagine life without them. They are everywhere. There is no total avoidance of them, only management of their irritant interruptions. I beg of you, be mindful of yourself and learn how to shut out their noise and to keep them out.

I've been told to sit down and tape up my mouth for it stank to high heavens because of the situations of birth. It came out of the fact that when my knees were parted, I was bestowed with a vagina and not a penis. The simple fact that it was a vagina meant that I was a reduced person and not allowed to share in the glories of life even when all life came through that passage. It was a testament of the subjugation of me out of the ignorance of the fact that Chukwu, the Almighty God, declared all creation and created good in His sight, resting on the seventh day. Here, there's no argument really, just a continuum of conversations.

Then came the prayer from mere men that said I should not be allowed to be seen and should remain unheard. An embargo of subjugation was placed at birth at the mention of me. 'She must be less,' they said. 'No!' they wailed, 'She is less, even less than a dog.'

But the story of Rebecca and Mma Eka is a tale of two different women.

Rebecca would have none of it. Rebecca fought for her child after her dead husband's kinsmen took her child away to the same man that defiled her just to spite her. In her moment of confusion, she had reached out to them, bearing tales of what had happened to Jabo and seeking solutions to what had happened to her only daughter. All in the name of culture, of the staining of family names and regaining of family values, they took Jabo back to her place of defilement, pain and torture. They had not forgotten her rejection of them, her being the very catalyst for their shame and pain anytime they saw her or were in her presence, even when she said nothing about their Nichodemus kind of visit to her, in her time of mourning and pain, in the dead of night. She had been silent about their visit of shame, so they had bided their time waiting for the turn of the tide.

They said she was a widow and had no say in family matters, but it was just Magnus, the elder brother to her late husband Agaba, trying to get his revenge. She fought and got her child back. She cleaned up her child and enrolled her in school, took care of her and consoled her. Like a hawk she watched over her. Ozoemena, our people will often name a child, meaning there should be no repetition. She never stepped foot in a church again. Rebecca closed that chapter of vulnerability in her life.

One day, people in her neighbourhood woke up and found the church of the man of God that defiled Rebecca's daughter Jabo burnt to ashes. The street had spoken and acted their judgement. No vile entity should be walking around their community. The man of God fled the area and no one saw him again. All the while, Rebecca kept mute. She maintained her territory and raised her children in silence, going about her business without a sound.

The day I saw her again, she brightened up. She said to me, 'nwanyi bu ife' meaning 'a woman is something of value'. My child's life is not one to be mortgaged. Her life will not stop because something repulsive happened to her. The story of Rebecca and her child is one of triumph and hope. Eventually, love won. I have learnt that this life has different dimensions to it. It's always about choices; you get to choose. Giving up my life is not one of the dimensions. Life will continue to be a matter of choice. How do I tell the tale of these two women? One refused to become a victim – she fought back, redeemed her child and gave her life back to her. She refused to be a wimp, she refused to back off and back down in the face of the evil and wickedness meted out to her and her child. She was denied justice but she stood up and fought.

Rebecca acknowledged that what had happened to her child was wrong. She was never in denial. She accepted that it was bad and that she was careless and too trusting of religious people and their allure. But she refused to fold her hands and accept that her child's life and future be ascertained and determined by the same man that had taken away her innocence, brought her pain, tore her soul to shreds and quickened her initiation into adulthood and adult ways. Agaba was indeed dead, but Rebecca took position and would wage war on behalf of her children. Nothing could faze her, not even this! They brought darkness into her bedroom and she ran towards the light. To take away her child's life would be to end hers. So she fought. She fought for life and not only regained it but won.

Nda's story with her child, on the other hand, is the tale of the proverbial fly that had no one to advise him and followed the corpse to the grave. When she dumped Eka with her own man of God, it elevated her to a high level of spiritual attainment. See no evil, hear no evil! Not for one day did she think about how this had destroyed her child. After Eka gave birth, she ran away. She had lost faith in her mother. Eka blamed her for what had happened to her. Her mother did not confront the man of God. She continued to worship in the church and serve as a 'worker' there. Even when she took Eka there, it was under the guise that prayers be made for her; she wanted her to be on 'holy ground' throughout her pregnancy.

Nda never told her man of God that she wanted him to take care of Eka. She never told him that she secretly wanted him to marry her even when he had a wife. The wife of the man of God was often seen around the church serving with the cloak of timidity around her. Nda was angry with what had happened to her child in private; she did not have the courage to confront the man publicly. She neither asked the man of God what happened to her child nor why he had done what he had to her. Instead, she made excuses for him. When he sent Eka back to her, she still did not ask questions nor challenge the man. Eka was bitter towards her and would often show it. So she ran away with her child after she gave birth.

Soon news began to filter to her mother that she was seen in a certain red-light district. Something happened to Eka in that church and as her pregnancy progressed; her situation became worse. Nda was asked by none other than the man of God that had defiled her daughter to come and remove her sick child from the church because she'd become a pollutant, possessed of demons, and prayers were no longer effective on her! Eka threw caution to the wind; it was her life, after all, and her mother never cared about her, though that was not really so. Her mother was blinded by religion. She was a prisoner of religion and its promoters.

One day, the daughter eventually came back to her mother after years and years of waiting for her return. Mma Eka was surprised to see a ghoulish figure approaching her house. It was in the evening, and she had just come back from her church. The church of her man of God. Even with the atrocities committed against her child, she stuck with the man and still fervently worshipped and served at the church. When Eka ran away, she took her child with her. Nobody knew why she would do that since it would have been easier to keep the child safe with her mother. I never asked the mother about the child, neither did I ask if the child was baptised and whose name it bore. I dreaded the answers and how they would increase my pains. My friend was wrapped up in the basket of religion, blinded by it, owned by it. She entertained no criticism.

All I've ever done was to support my friend even in the face of my own challenges. Often, she will remind me of my marriage-less life. And when I told her that I was not moved that way, she would fight and question if indeed it was Igbo blood that ran through my veins. She would shake her head and look at me in wonderment. She would say to me, 'You're a strange one. I can't understand you. Your people are not like this. Isi olu?' Meaning, 'are you from a foreign land?' I would laugh; this, my friend, is a good friend but saddled with the burden of pleasing men! But that story is not for today. I will tell it another day.

Nda told me that she saw the shadows of a woman approaching her compound with a child. A male child looking gaunt. When she said that, I remembered that in my sorrow of what befell Eka on the day she was brought back to her mother, heavily pregnant and very sick, after she gave birth I never bothered to ask the mother the sex of the child. It did not matter what sex the child was; all that mattered was how to rehabilitate Eka and restore her confidence and dignity. But then it seemed as if Eka was no longer interested in what mattered to her peers. Her sojourn in the hands of the prophet, her mother's man of God and the part her mother played, was a story she was not ready to tell. Something had happened to her there, but each time her mother broached the topic, she shut her down and would not talk about it. Often, she will respond by shivering and stuttering, which left her mother totally aghast and in tears.

They stealthily approached her premises and she stood up to go and meet them, these strangers, and to ask them who they were and whom they were looking for. As she watched them approach, she noticed that the lady struggled to walk. As she looked up, she saw some men quickly drop bags from a car and zoom off. Nda had not noticed the car. It then occurred to her that the car may actually have dropped those now walking into her compound. The boy child was almost in tatters and the woman looked so sick with dishevelled hair. She approached them cautiously.

When the lady was within reach, she whispered, 'Mma, I'm home.' She couldn't make out what she was saying and why she should address her as 'mother'. Nda looked at her quizzically and gasped as realisation dawned on her.

'Eka!' she gasped, 'is this you? Chukwubuife.' She quickly took the hands of the little child and brought them into the courtyard. Amadio! What do you say to this?

I heard about your recent appointment by the government. Wow! Your sojourn for the golden fleece has paid off. When you call me, remember that I'm confused. You speak high faulting English whilst you hold closed-door meetings with those who have collectively refused to guide us to light and give us life. You stack your bank accounts and line them up with the money which they pay you now as you advise them on the best way to handle our collective wealth and ruin us.

Amadio! Words leave me as I try to explain the agony of a woman whose child came back sick, without hope, without redemption. Is this the fate of our country? Are we without a future? Are we beyond redemption? I ask you. When you sit at those tables, remind them that it is indeed enough. Vultures gather over carcasses, but these are vultures of a certain kind. They do not wait for corpses; instead, they turn their people into them and prey and swoop on them. They are without mercy, bereft of conscience, blinded by their greed and their love for mammon.

On the day that Eka died, my phone rang whilst I was in the middle of work, grappling with melancholy, having signed off the job a long time ago. The voice I heard at the other end was surprisingly light, laden with sorrow but with an attempt to mask it. In it all, I detected a bit of relief and surrender. 'She's dead, Ifedi.' It was Nda, Mma Eka. 'Who is dead?' I asked. It did not register at first. 'Eka!' she said and dropped the line. I sat up from my desk like a bolt of lightning, arms across my chest. I went numb.

When Eka returned sick with a strange ailment, her mother tried all she could. She told me she was grateful that she was back. I thought she would be bitter because Eka had left without a forwarding address. She did not contact her mother all the time she was away. But Nda was happy that she was back and grateful in the face of it all and tried to nurse her the best she could graciously. I did not ask what the ailment was; I was not told. Much as I loved Nda, I needed to allow her to deal with this pain and sorrow on her own whilst lending support as much as I could.

There's always that personal space in dealing with life issues. Sometimes you have to allow people their personal, private space. It was her time to come into the realities of her actions and decisions towards her child. She would deal with it alone. I knew that my contributions would be sought later but my support was needed then and not necessarily my voice. So I kept my opinions to myself and gave my shoulders to her. Now this! I was in shock. My hands trembled a little. Such is life. I felt dizzy. It hit me so hard. I never expected it. I did not see it coming.

This life is full of complexities. I knew not to call back. I would go to my friend and console her and then let her grieve peacefully afterwards. She would need her space but I would be close by for the times when she needed my shoulders and someone to hold her hands.

"Chukwubuife!" she called as we sat in her courtyard. She still had mourning clothes on and I could see the freshly dug grave where finally Eka lay. I watched my friend play with her grandson and saw the glimpses of hope on her face despite the sorrow.

"It's not been easy," she said to me, "but as you can see, there's still light at the end of the tunnel."

I sat still as the evening wind blew gently around us from the guava tree.

"I never knew it would come to this. How do you have someone here with you and the next moment they are gone? How, Ifedi?" she questioned me. I allowed her to talk without responding because I did not want to add to her pains.

"In all of these things, I remain grateful. Yes, she died, but now I have a son who will carry on the name of this family." I looked at her sharply and wanted to remind her that this boy child would one day look for his father. The Igbo-ness, that blood in me, rose up! I spoke gently.

"But this boy does not belong here. You know that one day he will look for his father." His despicable father, I thought to myself. "When that day comes, what will you say to him?" I asked.

"Till then, till then," she nodded slowly in reaffirmation. "But now all I see is his bright future; through him, I can now hope. The future belongs to them," she continued. "The future belongs to those who hope and wait for it," she said finally.

"Really?" I quizzed, still angry at what had befallen Eka. I was alarmed at Nda placing the burdens of her hope on this child. There must not be a repetition of tragedy. Ozoemena! Eka died out of carelessness and I just couldn't get over it. Now you want to bet on this child? I thought furiously.

"The future cannot wait for you," I said hastily. "The future is here for the taking and for those who work for it and walk towards it now," I spat out. She ignored me. She knew I was still angry with her even if I refused to voice it. Being there at that moment was me just trying so hard to be nice and she knew it.

"Chukwubuife, come," she called out to her grandson. I could see the rapture in her face and the joy as he climbed onto her lap and curled up in her arms. Hers was a twisted story Bernard left because she had no son. Eka brought back a son to her. She seemed to sigh at that moment and cuddled him closely whilst she quickly looked at Eka's grave with misty eyes.

I thought about Chukwubuife's father, Nda's man of God, who after all these years has neither asked about Eka nor her child. In whose presence Nda receives prayers daily and whose words have become her mantra. Life is indeed strange. I kept my silence even when I had a lot of questions and anger still tugging at my mind. The man of God was an area of discussion forbidden between us. She had warned me in the past to keep off. I am still in pain at the effrontery and audacity of this man and the arrogant power he still wields over my friend. Until his blindfold over her is removed, nothing can be done to make her believe that an injustice took place. That this man destroyed the life of her child, betrayed her trust in him and was not called to justice. Still walking free as if nothing happened, even if she gained a grandchild, a son; it rumbles my stomach still. How do you explain these ironies of birth to this child when he begins to ask questions? Tell me how?

I looked at her and mellowed a bit. Nda had been through some sort of violence, abandonment, hardship, betrayal, and she was still standing. She, who married early, who thought she was in good hands, thought she was in it for the long haul, only to have her hope and her heart shattered into pieces. I had some sort of compassion at that moment for her. I had no right to judge her. I had seen her struggle through the trials and tribulations life had thrown at her, which could have buried another woman, and how despite some bad judgements and choices, she still gracefully continued to dress up and show up daily.

I reached out and held her hands. We sat in complete silence whilst Chukwubuife continued to banter the way only children know how to. Life can be shocking. The briefness of it is sometimes daunting. Yet we do not give up. We wake up daily and continue to trudge on fearlessly. Eka is gone but has left memories in Chukwubuife. No amount of tears and sorrow will be able to bring her back. Nda was happy to gain a son out of this tragedy and she was not going to bargain with this opportunity. There is a deep scar, a deep wound, with Eka's departure but there is the memory of a son. For Nda, it was the opportunity to rewrite a wrong she had allowed in the heat of carelessness, even if she refuses to accept her carelessness publicly. I know that privately she may have acknowledged her wrong to her child even if she continues to hold her prophet sacred. Eka's memory remains sacred and inviolable with her mother and expressed through her son. From the corners of my eyes, I saw deep lines beginning to crease her face and more around her eyes. I knew she'd gained them from sleepless nights and lonely days. Her eyes were beginning to regain their lustre and softness and I knew it came from this gift of a grandson, Chukwubuife. Sometimes you allow time. You allow time to do its work. Indeed, time changes yesterday. It changes everything.

There are days when I wake up to the uncertainty of it all to behold the wiles of what it means to become a woman in all its entirety. I was told that the day I came was an ordinary day without symbols. The only issue was the fact that what made me human was held in derision; it was held between my thighs. Hahaha! When I appear, world people will always judge my worth because of the mound between my legs. How salacious! To be born a woman in these climes was to come into disadvantage, almost a crime. It was to be held accountable for the follies and foolishness of society. I often wonder in my moments of reflection if it was worth it. When I'm raped, I'm condemned immediately because I caused it. You hear them ask, 'What was she wearing? How was she walking? How was she talking? What time of the day was it?' When a husband dies, the wife killed him. When a woman is divorced, she didn't try enough! She has failed!

Amadio, sometimes you ask me questions I cannot answer and stealthily you encroach in domains where you're not invited. You stay in the affront of strange places and claim dominion of a land which you have not mastered nor known the mysteries bestowed on it. How then can you ever proffer solutions to this country? How, Amadio? No roads, no schools, no hospitals, no housing, no jobs, no basic amenities, nothing at all! Our youths are stretched out on the streets without hope. The filth of our greed has enslaved us; daily we are blinded by it and daily it marinates us, making mincemeat out of us. We chew the diseased cud of abandonment, sorrowful and directionless leadership, indiscriminate looting and absolute lies every day. This life is a pot of beans.

Did you know that when Rebecca's daughter Jabo was asked what happened to the mound on her chest, she said it was chewed on by the man of God? The proverbial he-goat, the insatiable malefactor. Her torn pants an emblem of sacrilege. An abattoir of helplessness in the face of pervert adults with a penchant for the destruction of the future of young, budding hope, a decoy for the purity of the naive and unassuming. Their grandiose-acquired humility is on display for all to see, but they are wolves. Malevolent wolves! Even the discerning are often misled by their presentations of themselves. The streaks of dried tears on her cheeks were dry like the early winds of harmattan. The defiance of her response and her eyes, flat like fish on ice, brought a sigh to my lips and took the breath out of me. Rebecca, her mother stared in disbelief. She opened her mouth but no sound came out.

This is a tale of two women, Rebecca and Nda. The tale of two children, Eka and Jabo. The unpleasant tale of a country in recess. A story of anguish and the daily responsibilities of what it means to be born a woman in a world where men hold sway without compassion, without empathy, without shame, often brutal in action. Where they steal pure innocence in broad daylight. The narrative did not change nor did her attitude change; she was in shock. She had been preyed upon and her innocence sabotaged. The pause and the echo were in the same room at the same time but there was total silence. Jabo has been initiated into adulthood abruptly without her consent, without her permission. She was introduced to it as a thing of shame and guilt instead of an embrace of warmth and beauty. How in the world do we tell these stories? Stories shrouded in violence and held in darkness. I never thought in my entire existence that my bowels could stand the stench that hit my nose at the mention of what Jabo went through.

The silence of the elders at the communion of the women was the real awakening. She continued to stare whilst we looked at her lap filled with blood and her womanhood ripped apart, her innocence taken away from her. Rebecca opened her mouth again but no sound came out. She became moribund immediately.

She held her panties in her hand and her tears were dry like harmattan, her feet dirty, a half-eaten biscuit in her hand. How did we get here? How do you beat me and ask that I do not cry? The guttural sound from the mother could be heard. 'Afo one ka nwa a di! How old is this child? Gwa nu m oooo! You people should tell me,' wailed her mother, 'Kedu ife nwoke a na- acho n' ike nwatakilia, nnam oo. What is this man looking for in this child's vagina! My father, oo! He asked me to leave her in the church for prayers. Little did I know that it was just for him to destroy my life.' Rebecca continued to lament. 'So my child's blood-soaked pants and lap are the prayers said for her?' she asked. No one could console her.

You asked me to tell you what became of the church by the corner. The church of the man of God who wakes the neighbours up with his wails of damnation. The owner of a pulpit that ensnares women and rips people of their earnings whilst promising them utopia and Eldorado. A conman. You want me to tell you the stories of untruths taken not from the holy books but from the imaginations of deceitful and mean men. They often sell holy water and prayer books to the weak, the gullible, the sick, the thief and the wicked; even the mad man by the corner knows of their tricks. We woke up one morning and found that our child had been desecrated. We were dazed, we could not wail. They had our mouths covered.

How can it be said that the seer, the one that has God all to himself, is a lie and living a lie? Like a conman, he draws his willing subjects and feeds them with his lies and ensnares them. He keeps a veil over their eyes and minds; like a magician, he waves a wand over their brains and seals God in his pouch. He says, 'My father said I should tell you…' and we wonder if his father, the god, the deity, belongs to him alone. He seduces his subjects with promises of plenty but ends up stripping them of their life savings and their ability to think for themselves, even when his tricks are in plain sight. I hate religion without responsibility and conscience, piety without truth and empathy, passion without love and duty.

On the day that our sister is spoken for, what shall we do for her? We have a little sister and her breasts are not yet grown – Song of Solomon 8:8. It seemed like we looked on whilst she was ripped apart and her infant breast chewed on, her tender, innocent womanhood robbed, her maidenhood torn and lost forever. She has not attained the age where we would have spoken to ascertain if she's a door or a wall. Her virtue was stolen in broad daylight. Amadio, I hear you. The day after the next, you called and I told you to let me be. I told you to fear anything that has blood in its veins and stands as a man! 'Vipers,' I muttered under my breath. Vultures after carcasses.

I told you that men ensnare men and that, often times, you have to be powerful and divinely enabled to withstand the destruction that can come from another human. I told you that people die sometimes out of the choices they have made, sometimes from their inactions, and most times when their voices are silenced. I reminded you that when a man is castrated, he has nothing else to give the world. I heard you say 'eunuch' and I growled. I reminded you that I spoke not about physical castrations of impotency but the ability to have the power to change things but choose to stay inactive and look the other way. That's the real definition of impotency.

The voice that you silenced and the eyes you turned away when you had the chance to stand against evil and oppression count against you. Silence is poignant and a response heavier than speech. Remember to question your days of silence, remember to ask if it was worth it. There are times when silence is loud and there are days when it will take courage to remove the lid of silence and give out your voice. Those are the days when you beautifully stand in the shoes of others. Days when you become the voice of the voiceless. Better still, days when you speak against evil and call white, white and black, black.

I asked you why you ran away from this place. You said it was for greener pastures. Yet now you traverse both worlds as an advisor. I knew you lied then because you knew that the untruths embedded in these places can and will consume you. Amadio, stop telling lies! When you sit with them, please remember to tell them the truth! Be our burden-bearer! Our institutions are not working, our children may not see tomorrow. Our roads are contraptions. Our leaders are thoughtless. Our people are strangely silent, enjoying slavery and often times they say, 'Oh, we have the tenacity to withstand hardship.' Suffering and smiling. Those words.

Amadio, the time you were clinking glasses with the men that held us in captivity and slavery, I saw the smile on your face as I watched you on television. You have grown fat and your face shone so brightly, now rotund. You went into a closed-door meeting with them and came out with heavy pockets, even though you deny it. You say to me, 'Ifedi, I am trying to contribute my quota but it's best I do it from safety.' 'After all,' you say, 'this is my country and one day my children will still return to the land.' And I say to you, 'bravo.' I wonder, when you sit with your contractors, our 'big men', did you tell them about our 'educated' youths selling wares in traffic? Did you ask them to bring back health? What about education? What did they say, Amadio? When you spoke to them about the contraptions that have become our roads, did they clap your back and send you on your way as they always do? That's their attitude – nothing is urgent! Nothing matters.

Were you blinded by the effrontery of their ability to turn putridity into perfume? What did you say to them? How come you were not consumed by their hypocrisy? Did the aroma from their exotic dining block your nostrils from perceiving their lies? What happened? Amadio, did you help them plan their next campaigns with your recent fine learning and exotic speeches? Never in my life have I seen a man wear as many cloaks as you. The tears that fill my eyes do not drop. We have cried so many tears, but we sold out our lives to these people and, like prostitutes, we solemnly return to offer our bodies to them again and again.

They have us in a stranglehold. They know that we have no ability to unyoke ourselves from their snares. Year after year, they knock on our doors and we open our homes to them. We moan when they enter and sigh with relief when they leave, the greasiness of their vile deposits of destruction on our thighs dispersed for generations. They laugh, we cry. They stand, we fall. They have bounty, we have none. They live in exotic mansions; the squalor is our bed. They don't see us. They can't hear us. We are just instruments of war and divisions in their hands. We mean nothing.

They know we can never be satiated with their putridity, and like simpletons, we bay for more. Like leeches, they suck our blood to renew their strength. We've mortgaged our future and our lives. Like the evil cast of dark clouds on a lonely day, we pay obeisance to them.

Amadio! You have not done well! For truth is not found in your path. Your mouth is filled with a goblet of lies and your life is a testament of thievery and hypocrisy. You're like a lion that goes about looking for prey but wants me to see you like a lamb. Yesterday when you called, you accused me of not understanding the work you now do for our government, and I laughed. They need your acquired expertise, you say, but I say they need the truth more. Tell them the truth, though I can assure you they will not put it to good use. Very soon they will also wear you out. Eventually, you will pack up your expertise and go, unless you are ready to play their games. I suppose you may not, or will you?

Our friend Okanga called to say he's been relieved of his duties at the bank. On the day we met, I asked him if indeed he did his best on the job. I asked him if he put in his best and gave his best. But he was past caring. You remember how he used to scout the holes in Lagos looking for money? And how the banks, like slave masters, do not keep unprofitable slaves in their slave yards? He removed his tie and drank himself to a stupor, his eyes bloodshot and his palms sweaty as he staggered to his car, wondering how he would get home. I heard he plans to go to the country of the women whose children have sense and were sensible enough to build their country whilst they continue to pillage ours. The same place where you've found a safe haven.

Oh, Amadio, when you call, I shudder. Surprisingly, your calls are becoming empty and the ringtone very strange. How did you get to this point where you try to strangle words out of me? How strange that you call and then you begin your greetings with, 'Ifedinma, hello', high-pitched but filled with noise. Each time you call me, you pollute my ears and my space with noise. Do you not hear the rasping of my voice and the coldness of my musings? And then, my brisk, sharp answer: 'I wonder if you've forgotten how the struggle is.'

Every day in this world is a battle, but whilst others battle to improve on the good life they have in their climes, we battle to have life. Our battle is for our dignity every day. Our battle is for change, better change, every day. Our battle is for our lives and the lives of our children. Our battle is to make head and tail of the lies, the blatant abuse of power by these people, our leaders, every day.

Amadio, today I am at the hospital and the corridors are forlorn like a ghost town. We took Mbake to the hospital to deliver and we met no doctor on duty. It is the weekend: no doctors on duty in a federal hospital. They were on strike once again asking for better wages. Our hospitals have become sewages, voluptuous pits of hopelessness and darkness. It's very easy for one to walk in there with their two legs and leave in a casket. Our leaders don't find our hospitals appealing; they have found beautiful chattels in hospitals abroad. So when they are sick, with exchanges of foreign currencies they're whisked off to fancy hospitals abroad whilst we enjoy hospitals whose doctors are often overworked and always on strike demanding fair wages.

When a man is enslaved with iron bars on his feet, they say he is shackled, or manacled when his hands are tied behind his back. Tell me, when a man is enslaved by his own passion, fury, lust and inaction, does he not see that he is enslaved? How do you save him? When a man welcomes despair like a visitor, when a man entertains evil and makes a bed for wickedness, what do we call that? When a man makes a bed and invites his enemy to a feast and asks them to stay a while with him. When he makes conversation with these people and they look at each other from the corners of their eyes while frothing at the mouth, what do you call those?

Strange bedfellows? How do you contain lies when you tell them against yourself? How do you contain yourself when you're the one that brought ant-infested lizards into your home and unto yourself? Why do we eat indignities and birth evil with urgency? Even when we laugh, the emptiness shows in our eyes and mocks us.

We talk about our future, the future. Yet the legacies we're breeding mock the pictures of the future we're painting.

It is indeed men that divide men. It is men indeed that spoil good things. We create opportunities for chaos and malaise. We create pools of sadness and yet turn round in bewilderment and wonder at our apocalypse. Life is worth living. Love is worth experiencing in its raw form. Why do we shut our ears to reason and reasoning and stand astonished, shocked by the utter mockery and in wonderment of the creation of such chaos? Why are we disgusted at the sight of the ripples created by our selfishness, wimps and caprices? Why are we surprised at the results of our hate and that of our wickedness? Why do we hide when our actions are x-rayed and we show pretences of shyness and mockery of repentance?

We are bewildered at the racy pulses and actions of men when they behold power and of women when power is laid before them. What sarcasms of ineptitude escape our lips when we try to undermine and deny the injuries inflicted on others by the irresponsible power laid bare before our eyes? Why do we run in the face of the consequences of our hypocrisy, even though when it was time to speak out against evil, our lips were sealed with metal gongs and our eyes glazed with the mistiness of our evil aspirations? We dare not speak against those that have driven us to our knees because we wait our turn. We dare not speak against them because they are our kith and kin. We dare not speak against them because we belong to the same party whilst the truth is orphaned, the country on the brink. It is the national cake; it belongs to everybody but nobody. The goat owned by the community will often starve to death. The country is on the edge with cracks in the wall, yet we still say it is turn by turn instead of demanding for true leadership with accountability.

Any nation that leads without accountability is dead on arrival. It might as well be a ghost town. It is a country where men and women live and die in anarchy.

When you refused to allow justice to reign, what was it you were thinking? Where nepotism is rife, what do you expect? Where there is no meritocracy, what else do you lean on? You cannot plant yam and harvest tomatoes. It is against the natural order. But the world is in revulsion of the natural order. There are a lot of new introductions in the world today and they are often strange. There are whispers about these strange new things and you are asked not to ask questions. Not to judge, just accept.

Amadio, I chewed my lip and gnashed my teeth. Mbake's baby came stillbirth and Mbake lost the struggle. Please! When you ring again, don't drop the call like your phone has become hot with tantalum mined in blood in Congo. I hear your mirthless laugh. Have you been to Congo? Why does humanity enslave humanity? What goes up comes down. What goes around comes around. The blood mined in Congo rests on the conscience of the world. What is the acquisition of wealth without morality? But I digress.

In the year that our daughter is spoken for, she must be a wall. If she is a wall, we will build towers of silver on her. If she is a door, we will enclose her with panels of cedars. Song of Solomon 8:9. The veracity of womanhood and being a woman is embedded in her implicit faith to nurture humanity. The abominations and rape done to her have created unrest. Where is your conscience? What is your morality? We have sucked out the ability of this womanhood to rise up and take her proper place. Often, we have lowered her dignity from a point of contact for prosperity and life to a place of shame. We come, we live, and then we depart.

Amadio, I know one thing; we are wayfarers and nothing lasts forever. We preach love with one corner of our mouth whilst we deal out hate from the other. We close the doors of real living and life with our embellishments of falsehood and our silence, echoing agreement. We cry tears of hypocrisy when we are destroyed by the same contraptions we created by our collective silence in the face of robbery and thievery. When we see these men, our slave masters, we orgasm and rejoice. We salute them warmly and ask them when they are going to visit us again. We watch as they pass the baton of idleness, despair and hopelessness to us and our children. We curtsy and bow before them and kiss their rings. We watch as their children take the baton. We see that they've become more fierce, more wicked and more evil than their forebears. We cry in loneliness when they depart from us, and once they reappear, we use our rags to adorn their paths as a testament to our loyalty. 'When the pupil is ready, the teacher will appear' is a very profound saying. We are not ready yet. We deserve the governance we have. We love our captors more than we do ourselves. We empower them daily. We have energised them and there is no going back. They have tasted the honey and now they cannot let go.

Amadio! You have become a contractor. I see you now decked in fineries, your lips smooth and filled with fine wine and lies. You have joined them but vehemently you deny it. You say you're still part of the struggle and you have now become a nation-builder, but I am no longer sure what you are or what you've become. The phone calls are becoming infrequent and you are always in a hurry when you call. When I raised my concerns, you said to me, 'Ifedinma, stop being paranoid. I can work for the government without being corrupt.' You tried to reassure me. 'Besides, I am only in an advisor capacity,' you said. 'They may or may not take my advice and this I can tell you is what has happened.' I shrug it off. You alone know the truth and what the truth looks like, Amadio. It's only the truth that sets one free.

You laughed and said I reminded you of how I was back in school. Always pushing for clarity and demanding that my friends stay on the good path. Amadio, we've been friends for so long. Working with our government when you have a name to protect is like walking on a landmine. I hope you will be able to walk that path. I don't know anybody who comes to them with the truth that survived them without scars. Unless you do not have a name to protect. You gave your assurances, but I am no longer sure. You're beginning to sound like them and I am awash with paranoia on your behalf. You asked me again about Rebecca and what became of her. Rebecca's story is still one that I do not enjoy telling but again it is one that shines the light on the hope and redemption that love can bring. Rebecca is a truth-teller. This is my summation of her. She is brave. It takes bravery and courage to tell hard truths to yourself and acknowledge where you have messed up. Rebecca did not hide away from the truth. She embraced it and sought healing for herself and Jabo.

They held Rebecca responsible for Jabo's pains. The women came together and they slapped a fine on her.

The day that I went to see her, she sat on the pavement looking like someone who was lost. I called out to her. When she saw that it was me, she hid her face. Rebecca's eyes were sore with crying and red like henna. I went to her and held her. I knew she still hurts. It was not only the loss of her child's innocence but also the conflict of the community and the pointing of fingers. The redirecting her back to culture and her state as a woman, especially a widowed woman. Her pain, she told me, starts in the morning and does not ebb when she lays in the silence of the darkness in her room at night, alone with guilt in remembrance of what was done to her child.

Rebecca asked me questions, half of which I had no answers to, for how do you ask me questions for the gods? How do I ascertain answers from mysterious places? She told me that her daughter's life was taken away from her forcefully and the man was still gallivanting around in white robes. She hissed and spat on the sand. When she raised her eyes to me, I saw that they were distant; she did not see me at all.

"Where is Jabo?" I asked. She let out a tense tear, looked at me with outstretched hands, then spoke slowly. The men of the family had decided to take her away. Her uncle Magnus gave her to the man of God to mend what he had destroyed. I stared at her in horror. I screamed but no sound came out. I thought I had been rendered useless at that point.

I stammered out the words, "But how could that be?" I shuddered. I felt like I had been punched in my stomach. I was breathless for a while, then from afar, I heard her whisper.

"They took her away to the prophet to remedy her." I thought I had heard that before. It sounded familiar. "Culture demands that," she said in a high-pitched voice and laughed crazily, not believing her own words.

The enormity of the inabilities bequeathed to women came slowly like a shroud around me. I felt a slight, breezy cold and I had goosebumps at the ability of society to clamp the mouths of women. The ability of women to also create the opportunities for the oppression of fellow women by men. The ability of women to become accomplices, complicit enablers, whilst crying wolf. I was stunned by the actualisation of the enrapture of subjugation of another soul through social vehicles of isolation, deprivation and sick cultural orientations. I wept then in the realisation of the loss bequeathed to Rebecca, of the enormity of the evil done to Jabo and her mother, of the emptiness of it all.

"It has always been like that." I heard her from a distance. "They have to decide, you know." Then she spat out the words. "I'm only a woman. I'm also a widow." Rebecca tried to cajole me to accept the depravity of it all, but the injustice that weighed on my soul would not allow me to accept a lie. It was like a block of cement tied to my soul, yoked to my neck.

"Thunder fire Satan." I provoked like the average Nigerian. She sobbed in the wanton emptiness of her loss and bereavement.

"They said he should put her back the same way he met her or marry her and take care of her needs since he defiled her."

"And what did you say, Rebecca?" I looked at her in bewilderment. "How can you live with this? How is it that you cannot fight for your daughter? How did you release her to the same man that raped her, took away her innocence and blackened her soul? A ten-year-old child." My blood boiled at the thought of this child being there alone. I wept at the depth of this evil and the corruption of the souls of men.

We are just wayfarers on this earth, sojourners with limited time on our hands. Sometimes it's blurry, some days we are quickened and awakened. Often times, we are afraid to live out our truth. Some days, we are bold in the face of our enemies and nemeses. Other days, we withdraw into our cocoon chewing on the fabrics of our loneliness. When there's confusion, where is the reasoning in the clutter? How do we escape even the semblance of peace laced with audacious lies and thievery? For such delivery and embrace of peace will eventually implode. We have to come to the place of acceptance that no matter how you try to convince another person to fight for life, such people should be left to find their own measure of deliverance. They must be allowed to approach their freedom and deliverance on their own terms. They must find their path personally. They must be allowed to negotiate it however they want.

As I stood and looked at Rebecca, I shuddered at life's ability to strip a man, more so a woman, of the ability to have absolute control over the outcomes of their life. Extensions of families can sometimes be depriving, meddlesome and can bring confusion and destruction if care is not taken. It also depends on how it is managed. Life can indeed strip people of the ability to approach living by their own terms, however they want to. I know we would like to argue that any man can forge his path, but I ask in wonderment how it is so that bad things can still happen to good people and that bad people still roam the streets brazenly. We can plot, we can plan, but I believe utterly in outside influences.

I believe in the power that belongs to Chiokike alone, the Almighty God, the one that has absolute control over all things. No matter how clairvoyant you are, you cannot predict entirely where you will be the next moment or how your life journey will end. I believe that life must be lived with a great deal of faith and belief that things will be alright in the end. We must urgently speak our truth and live a life that is not harmful to the next person. But life in this world is filled with ironies and metaphors, the right-wing and the left-wing. The politically correct and the straight-shooters. The liars, the murderers and what have you. Collective robbers of people's destinies, dimwits and their cohorts.

I stared at the endless space in front of me, then I felt her nudge me.

"It's late," she said, "won't you come inside?"

I asked her knowingly, "How do you feel?" Slowly, she stared at me with bloodshot eyes. "I feel nothing. I feel nothing!" she declared and whispered in a hoarse voice. She got up from the pavement and walked away.

I felt ambushed. No child should experience this horror.

I suddenly felt cold and lonely. Another child's innocence had been taken even before her life had begun. Her mother's breath cut short and her life stifled; she was rendered powerless. She dies daily, knowing that her only girl child is held by a culture in the gulag of the same man who destroyed her life.

"Ife ukwu jetalu," said her own mother Ijele. "With her own legs she walked into trouble," she reiterated. To Ijele, Rebecca had no business going to that church. She shouldn't have trusted anybody with her girl child.

Rebecca's quest to receive prayers consumed her only daughter. Rebecca lost her husband and thereafter sought succour in the church. Each time she passes by a home of prayer, how does she react? I pondered. Does their hypocrisy twist her stomach? What mayhem do they unleash on her whenever she hears their loudspeakers? Does she shudder when she remembers the lap of her daughter splattered with blood, her hymen torn from her, her womanhood robbed from her, her innocence defiled and twisted? When she remembers Jabo, her daughter, how she lifted her eyes to her and said boldly, 'He chewed on my breast and put 'his thing' in my vagina,' does she blindly rage? What does she do? Is she limp and silent, wishing it away like an echo?

I shouted at her through my spirit, at her shadows; my soul took voice. 'Rebecca, you're a coward. Rebecca, go and retrieve your child from the monster, your pastor, your man of God whom you've allowed to destroy your daughter. Rebecca, go and salvage what is left of your dignity. Rebecca, your silence is ominous and it will kill you. Don't stay in your house and do nothing. Stop acting like you're impotent. Rebecca, go and salvage your child or you will live in shame for the rest of your life.'

What sort of retributive justice is Magnus, her late husband's brother, trying to conjure? How sincere is he in getting justice for his niece? What exactly is the name of this dance? Why did he not involve the law? Why do we always keep quiet in the face of rape and resort to shame and shaming the victims? How will the evil man restore what he stole forcefully? Will taking her back restore her hymen and her dignity? Was it just a way for Magnus to take his pound of flesh for his torn ego? What was it? Is it a reminder that she is a woman and therefore must recognise her place and assume it, no matter her attainment and accomplishments as a person?

Rebecca gave Magnus twenty-four hours to return her child but I told her not to wait for him. Go and get your child. The deed is done. You alone can fight for yourself. Don't let them deceive you into believing that they are fighting for the wrong done to your child because they are not. They are reclaiming their dashed egos, stamping their vengeance for your refusal of them. They did not forget your 'no' to their fleshly lust. They booked a day for your payback and the day is here. Don't allow the smirk on their faces to linger. Wipe it off by taking your child back. Give them no satisfaction by being subdued. Rise up in quiet strength and regain your life with no apologies. Once there is life, there is hope, and we must grasp it.

How do we stand here and pretend like we are mute, deaf and blind at the same time? Why do we lie and hurt ourselves? The day is done and night is upon us, yet we blindly grope in the dark pretending not to hear the voice of haste in the dark, asking that we turn on the light. Why do we cry when people die? Is it to assuage our own feelings that soon it will be our turn? What is it in that moment when we let go of our heart and tears rain down? What does it mean at that point? A loneliness, a stretch of the imagination, that shows us our humanity and a reminder that nothing lasts forever. I can't imagine the death that occurs whilst one is still alive, the one that is called the 'living death'. To witness this kind of death is horrible.

Rebecca is a living dead without her child; she knows she

is alive but dead and that's all I can say. How do I tell this story, on what premise? What argument, what reasoning, can she say made her relinquish her daughter to Magnus, her late husband's brother? Why did she allow them to take her child to a mad man, her tormentor, a robber of innocence? Was she blinded by the throes of the bereavement she was already going through, or by helplessness? Was that why she allowed them to take her child back to a man laced in the fabrics of madness and devilry without conscience, totally devoid of humanness? What is life?

Amadio, life is good for you. Every time you call me now, you sound grandiose. In the wake of your questioning, I hear you smirk. I feel like you know you have arrived and all the time you speak in borrowed tongues I hear your mockery of me. When I drop the phone, I get mad, so mad at what you represent. I wonder how you sit at those tables at those conferences and listen to lies. How do you people find company with lies? On the day that Rebecca died, I knew then what it meant to be alive and still dead, wholly rotten inside. I knew then that taste of rotten teeth when you open your mouth and the first gush of air out of it has this putrid smell and taste to it, and you wonder why your neighbour has suddenly moved her face a bit away from you to evade the stench.

Amadio, when you called, I was not myself. I thought about this pain, this pain that had drilled a hole into Rebecca's heart. I was restless, staring at the ceiling, counting the cobwebs. As I stared, I remembered how we played swell when we were young. I could hear again our shrills of excitement and how we would share 'chop one and chop two' with our dirty hands. 'The years of innocence,' we both said, reminiscing. I remember those years fondly. Amadio, truthfully, some days when life presents its hardness, I go back and hide in the memories of our pleasant childhood. You laughed beautifully when I said this to you and there was a memory of silence between us.

How is it that in this journey of life there seems to be lots of mysteries one cannot unravel? How is it that in this journey sometimes there's a strangeness to it? And how is it that most times life comes with its own twisted challenges? One day, you're certain you can brave it. Other days, your curtains are drawn, you're curled up like a ball in a dark room on a windy, creaky bed, never wanting to step your feet on the floor and go face the world. This is how I feel right now, Amadio, my friend. Why does it sometimes feel as if life and living are like a bad dream that one needs to wake up from? I thought about Jabo; how dare he violate the innocence still at its wake? How dare he lure this little girl to his den of robbery and take advantage of her future without her permission? What will make him undress in front of this child and scatter her life? They say time heals all wounds; I say, tah like a chameleon time changes colour.

I do not believe that time heals all wounds – that is a blanket statement. I believe that some wounds may mellow with time. Some days, they may stab at the heart gently, while on other days, they may stab with a bang. They may not totally fade away and heal. There always will be reminders and remnants, even residues. What eventually changes might be your reactions to a wound. It all depends on how deep and how strong it was in the first place. Like an amoeba, time is intertwined by experiences exuded and most times they evolve. We either become wiser, retarded, numb or consumed by what happens to us. Sometimes there are miscarriages of destinies along the path of this life. There are yokes that abort our destinies and keep us crippled and dazed without understanding. This life, my brother, is a pot of beans. We clap, we dance, we sing, we cast our glance about us and like warriors of the night we seek answers. Sometimes there are glimpses of hope and other times a dead end, a stalemate.

Amadio, if you call, remember that these places were not meant to be fallow. These places were meant to be fertile, green and full of life. These places were meant to be custodians of values, hope and redemption. These places were meant to be places of refuge. Amadio! When you call, remember the green-white-green. It was meant to be a place of pride. We were meant to stand in front of it with our chests laden with pride and our faces glowing with smiles and its draperies on our shoulders. We were meant to be children of the future, bearing hope and goodwill to others. But now we are the rejects of the earth. Why do we mourn and laugh at the same time? Why do we heave and wink with the corners of our eyes? Why do we unleash soldier ants on our newborn babies with their umbilical cords tied to sorrow? Why do we cry and at the same time unlatch the doors so that our women and children are taken as spoils of war? Why do we pretend when they finally come to our homestead to deposit their waste? Why do we show our rotten teeth and grin whilst white spittle spreads from the corners of our mouth in pain, hunger and lack?

I have never known a man so bereft of wisdom like you, or is it pretence? You say I always take out my frustrations on you whenever you call. Maybe you are right. Maybe I am envious of the relative peace and calm you now enjoy. The way you have worked out your life and made it foolproof irks me. This journey of life was meant to be lived with dignity, but alas, we've chosen the path of death and everything in between. We've held ourselves in prisons, yet we are here wondering why the gates are locked. Standing here looking at myself, I feel aloof, withdrawn from this place. Unattached to it in a surreal way. I feel the surgical untangling from this place and the hopes of our romance turning into a commitment of a lifetime dashed. Yet I hope. My heart is heavy, my soul laden with pain. I can't see the future. The future screams bleak, bleak, bleak.

As I try to see, my eyes become blurry with mist in front of me. It will be the death of me to watch my life taken away from me by cowards who move in droves because they cannot stand alone. Collectively they meet in the deep night, then in the wee hours of daylight they escape into the world to wreak more havoc. They think they've won, but the more I look at them, the more I see their maggot-filled buttocks. The more I look at them, the more I see their rotten souls. The more they hide their leprosy, the more their clothes are soiled by the pus from their rotten wounds. 'O ji onye, ji onwe ya', that Igbo adage. 'When you hold a man in grips, you're holding yourself. Until you release him you will never be free.'

The more I look at myself, the more I see the suffering, the melancholy of it all. The dreams frittered away by mean men. The cries of the future generations on the street side. The lack of empathy by the rulers and the wickedness of it all. The brazenness of the thievery, the collective robbery of the vast future that belongs to all of us. Weep not, child! This is a satire! The youths are trying to escape the irony of the gulag in strange ways. Vultures of a certain kind. The white man's mentality of the black man will not change and the black man's mentality of the white man neither. It will always be mired in suspicion. Understanding and assumptions have nothing to do with skin colour. It is a personal journey of discovery. The intrigue remains. The possibility of a man allowing the intricacies of another man to exist, sans cultural disposition and natural environment, is still a conversation today. Live and let live! The more I seek to understand it, the more confused I become.

There is this complexity of opinions that jars at my innermost person when a man selfishly wants to hold another man captive and subtly moves towards it. Don't hold a man on what you know or have heard of him; rather, hold a man by your true experiences of him. The hypocrisy of looking at a fellow on the surface, the beautiful smiles belying a dark soul, a dark loathing, a secret life of judging him or her on the premise of prejudice, is unimaginable. I've always wondered why men cannot take the simplicity of the creation, diversities and differences in life and run with it. Sometimes even the one that posits charity and understanding does so out of selfishness. It's a wonder what a man can become. The rawness of hate and destruction of man to man often leaves me stupefied, in awe and in amazement. I used to wonder at the nonsense that life often dishes out.

I'm amazed at how women scream gender equality but often, when in touch with power, still exclude their fellow women. Yes, I said it! I wish to ask women to be truthful in their approach and their request, even as I stand against discriminations meted out to us and the various distortions of images representative of women. I wish that there was no hypocrisy or greed at the bottom of our solicitations, that instead we advocate only truth. 'He who must come to equity must come with clean hands.' I wish to ask them to actually be the real voices of change.

Tell me, dear Amadio, I ask who else has access to these powerful men? Where do they lay at night and who do they wake up with? I'm tired of debates. I'm tired of meetings, conversations, negotiations and conferences without results and true change.

When we want to act, let's act truly, and when we want to speak, let it be with simplicity and truth.

There are days when I thought I would close my eyes and it would all go away. The pains of bad leadership, the wilful pillaging of a country's resources. The reduction of our powers to be great to the debris of corruption. The emancipation and amalgamation of hate, falsehood and deceit. The crave for eternal powers, ancestors holding onto power to their deathbeds, the casting of slavery chains on our necks by our rulers. This place called country, my fatherland, has long lost its meaning and appeal.

When I hear the voices of the children, I wonder to myself, how long? How long will it take my country, my nation, to realise that enough should just be enough? The cries of the victims of evil leadership go up to heaven every day. How is it that we plunder our now, plunder our future and wonder at the darkness that's taken our souls captive? When we blame these men and ask for the entrails of the chicken whilst the meaty part roasts on the fire, I know firmly in my soul that we are accomplices. I wonder at the level of our complicity and my eyeballs go large as if they will burst from their sockets.

Don't blame the children whose mothers made sure to teach them how to act and how to take care of their land properly so that tomorrow will be kind to them. Blame the darkness of the soul of your brother, who even though he knows that life is mortal, still thinks he's immortal. Blame your brother who thinks he's indestructible but will be ruined in one fell swoop. When the moon is lit and the hyenas bay and bark and you hear the crickets call, remember to shake your head at the evils that have been thrown up on the land, your land, by your brothers. Remember to mourn the darkness you wake up to and which you often embrace when you lay down.

These people's consciences have been seared and sealed with hot irons; there is no going back. Unless a grain of wheat dies, it will not live again, nor will it sprout to its full stature. The old must give way for the new, but it refuses to give way. They continue being recycled even though they are worn and of no use again to anybody, not even to themselves. How much is too much? We often forget to ask when we lie and turn our eyes to face away from the truth. Who then can help us?

Amadio! Remember that the question you ask has answers, but we've refused to use the answers even when they're in plain sight because they do not pay us. They have put a knife to what held us together and put our teeth on the edge. We are no longer at ease. We have become a country pregnant with chaos and confusion. When others run to the light, we run to darkness. We embrace it and grovel in it.

Today is just one of those days when it seems as if the throes of the suffering of the common man have hit the streets of heaven. They killed the youths in droves and made an abattoir of their blood. Sleaze is on display in the streets along with the cries of the youngsters who have taken flight with heavenly wings.

It seems that the morning is here because men in police clothes will not let the young people be and the youths have awoken from sleep. The harassment of them and the refusal of these youths to let it be business as usual, whose futures have been stolen and shared by these men, these bloodthirsty politicians, has taken them to the streets to protest an end to this evil, this evil government and governance.

Hahaha, hehehe! I heard the spirits laugh and it was empty and eerie as the crossroads between the living and the dead merged. What a gory sight, what a sorry state. How long is too long for the liberation of this nation from the hands of thirsty, bloodsucking, gusty men? They turned their guns on them and mowed them down and silenced their voices of demand. How dare they! What impetus! What audacity! How long shall women continue to return home to these dusty, dark places, their children slain, their clothes soaked with blood? When will liberation and freedom come?

The worst state of a man is to be left in fetters and shackles whilst hallucinating to be free. Freedom is costly and the ability to hold speech and give it out freely is very liberating and grandiose, but it comes at a price. To have a voice is to have everything. To be heard is very precious. Until your voice is lost, you will never, ever reckon with this.

Until you're muzzled, you will not be thankful for the gift of free speech.

So I remember the activists, those whose consciences are seared with wanton gluttony, whose attitude is one of settlement. 'Settle me with the national cake and buy my silence forever.' An ode to Fela. I laugh now as I remember, in a haze-like mode, his voice of warning. I hear him now: 'Dem be thief! Beast of no nation!' Fela preached, he sang. We did not hear. He even went to prison! Hahaha, hehehe! I heard him laugh. He called our attention to them, but we were busy sleeping. I sigh. They go into chambers of negotiation dressed in certain robes and re-emerge with others. They trade their conscience with filthy lucre and bare their teeth in a mockery of those who sent them, hoping that the scent of their deceptions are not perceived, nor their change of robes deciphered. They are part of our problems. Their negotiations of us and the settlement of them. Their doublespeak. Their knowing where all the bodies are buried. Today is not about them. I have no time to remember them today. Every man has a price. What is yours? Can you name it boldly?

Sometimes when I hear my name called out, I remember the

reason why I love my name. My name Ifedinma means 'This is a good thing' but its interpretation relies on its pronunciation. It could still mean 'Things should be well'. But this is my name and I'm still alive in the wake of all this hopelessness. To be a woman even in this present time is Herculean and an uphill task. To be totally defined by my country and be assessed by all it stands for and profits from is certainly so unfair. But a man and where he comes from are like two peas in a pod. How do you explain that you are different from your environment and that the nurturing of you and the essence of who you've become has nothing to do with who your country is and what your country has become?

The emblem of your country becomes your trademark; you're first a Nigerian before you can claim that you're Igbo. And when my identity is in question, I go to the mirror and ask questions of what I see. I can gladly tell you that I've never been in doubt of who I am and where I am coming from. For even before I start to claim my country, I am first and foremost of the Igbo stock. The blood in me does not lie; it reminds me daily of what it took to be me and the ancestry that runs through my veins. It's tough to be Nigerian, but how do I explain to you, my dear, that even in the hopelessness that has become my country, I'm still proud of my heritage? For it seems that we are of a warrior stock, confused by the amalgamation of us, yet it is that ugliness that seems to define us, that has made us stronger in the face of various adversities.

There's a certain kind of untruth always found amongst some rulers of countries. There's a certain kind of common falsehood which they drink and become full of. There seems to be this evil cloak which some rulers put on when they ascend the thrones of their country, but I say to you once again, even though you've heard it often: there's no honour amongst thieves. Have you noticed how some rulers lie and lie and often ad-lib and leave their country glitched? Their country's human lives are wasted and laid bare on the altar of lies. But not all of them. There are rulers that will lay down their lives for the honour of their countries. Their nationals fly their flags with pride. For my country, I pray for benevolence and deliverance someday.

Have you seen the hypocrisy of nations and governance? Though some seem to be worse than others. Buy me a handkerchief, let me cry you a river. Have you seen how lives are thrown on a chessboard by these rulers of men? Whilst they hold goblets of wanton destruction to their lips. How do we cry? Do we cry at the early hours of dawn or at the wake of dusk? Tell me, how do we lament and how do we open our mouths to wail? Do we even know what time to lament, or do we just turn away limply and accept our fate? Pray, tell me! It makes me look at the life of a woman again and again. The continual reliance of a woman and her sum total on a man whilst obliterating her entire existence by herself; is that how she should live her life? What's her essence? Must she be subjugated by the very same society she helped bring her birth? I only asked a question and sought answers.

My mind goes back to Rebecca and her daughter. Must the sum total of her existence and that of her child be dependent on the male members of her family? Rebecca did not make excuses. She told me she had no luxury of excuses. A woman has to do what she has to do. The same emblem of widowhood cast on her, she told me, had awoken a strong volcano for survival. Rebecca said that the death of her husband forced her to take stock and gave her the power to stand up for herself. She told me that she had begun to take self-preservation seriously after her husband Agaba died. Then she spoke about the sanctity of the church and how it no longer made sense to her.

I asked her on one of those days if she still believed in Chukwu, the big God. She looked at me and laughed. She asked me if it's possible to extract air with hands, and I said no. 'Then that is how impossible it is for me to stop believing in my chi,' she said to me. I still would often wonder at her and the seeming removal of the male cover from her by the death of her husband, as supposed by our culture and her exposure to wolves, lone wanderers and lonely, audacious, malicious marauders of the fleshly type; malefactors.

I am beguiled by the irony of our religion, how men have taken positions of God and how they've been able to lay traps for the vulnerable. Rebecca had excused herself from the church and its practices because of these ironies and inconsistencies. I wonder at the incursion of our country people, men and women in 'the service of God', and how they have become 'soul winners' for Him, but have actually denied thirsty people looking for God real access to Him.

They have become negotiators between God and men.

I will always remember that even in the Igbo parlance, the spiritual journey is not communal – it is always a personal journey. That, most times when a person is going through difficulties or challenges, the agbala will inquire from their chi their personal 'gods' on their behalf. What, then, is this display of the ignoramus type in the face of religion and its promoters? Rebecca told me that her soul had been broken into pieces by her hunger and thirst for solace in the church. Now that she has found herself, she has removed her eyes from the church and its penchant for obvious entrapment of the souls of men and the control of it.

PART 2

Rebecca was wise; she knew not to argue with evil men, the same men that had abandoned her when her husband died. She told of the day her husband was buried; how the elder brother Magnus had crept into her mourning room. She was aghast, trembling as she lay in the pitch darkness in deep mourning, remembering how the man with whom she had shared her life had died on the terrible gulag called Federal Government Road on his way to Maiduguri to buy fish.

Agaba had been trading in fish for fifteen years. He was a kind man, quiet, unassuming – a provider in the true sense of the word. It was a bright morning when he died. Rebecca never expected it. She was busy getting ready to go to Ajani Mobiles where she worked as an administrator. But she was unsettled. Something was going on in her stomach and she had gone to use the toilet that morning more than five times. It was unlike Agaba not to call. She heard the ticking table clock on her room desk from the passageway where she stood trying to get into her shoes. It was unusually loud, she thought. They had spoken the night before and he was in high spirits. Yet it was unlike him not to call. She got her things ready for work quietly, yet there seemed to be a log of wood tied to her legs; it felt so heavy that, for a second, her legs froze and she was immobile. The children had left for school. As she moved about trying to organise and plan her way to work, she quietly observed the time. She reached for her phone already in her bag but shrugged it off.

"I will call when I get to the office," she muttered under her breath. Maybe his phone is dead, she reasoned. Rebecca, stop overthinking, leave well enough alone, she chided herself. She left.

Whilst on the road, her phone rang.

"Rebecca?" the voice on the other end asked, "Where are you?" It was her husband's elder brother Magnus. They'd not spoken for months and she wondered why he was calling her so early in the morning.

"I'm on my way to work," she answered. She noted a tone of urgency and desperation in his voice but she shrugged it off.

"Can you come back please, there are some documents I need from your husband for the work I'm handling for him regarding the warehouse he's building at Ajamgbadi."Rebecca was taken aback. Agaba had not told her about this project. Quite unlike him not to tell me, she thought.

"Bro Magnus, can't it wait?" she asked. "I'm almost late to work."

"Please come back, Nne. I really need those documents."

Nne, she thought. He had never addressed me like that before.

"You know how those area boys around that area behave," he continued. "I need to check some things with the contractor and the site engineer. I need those papers and it's urgent."

Which papers? she thought. They had land for development in that axis, but Agaba said he was not ready to do anything on the land for now. Did it mean he had started work on the land without letting her know? 'Well let me go home first,' she said to herself. Magnus would not call unless something was going on.

"Ok," she said to him, "Let me call the office to let them know I will be late to work."

She made the calls and turned back. She called Agaba's phone again and it was switched off. Strange, she thought. Eventually, she approached their compound; she knew that something was wrong. People were gathering in a cluster whispering in low tones. They saw her and fell silent. Most of her husband's family members living in Lagos were there. From the corner of her eye, she saw her husband's elder brother Magnus walk towards her. Her heart was beating so fast, almost jumping out of her mouth, then she knew. She was numb, shivering and afraid. A weird feeling overwhelmed her.

He led her to a seat gently and calmly without speaking. The women began to approach her, at first in a hesitant manner, then hurriedly, most of them crying, their eyes red until they sat around her on the floor. Rebecca raised her head and laughed wildly. As she made to stand from where she was sitting, the earth swirled around her. The women held her down. She sat with her head jerked backwards, her eyes half-open, observing the neighbours trooping in. This is the end of the journey, she thought. She laughed again. Agaba, so this is it! This is why you did not call. This is why you did not come back. She laughed again maniacally with her arms across her bosom.

Life can take a turn and a twist in a twinkling. There are no guarantees, none at all. Your life can go from zero to a hundred in a second and from a hundred to zero in a minute.

"Where is Agaba?" she finally asked. Palpable silence at first, then sniffing from the women around. "Magnus," she asked, "where is my husband?"

"He is on his way back," he answered, his eyes averted, his eyes red.

"But why are all these people here? Are they crying just because he is on his way back?" she asked in a low tone, jeering at him, mocking him. "What are they doing here?" She turned her neck straight to him and slightly slanted it to observe him. She steadily stared at him without blinking, demanding the truth from him.

He sighed. "Agaba had an accident this morning on his way back."

She let out a loud laugh in a demented way. "So where is he? Where did he have the accident and which mortuary did they deposit him?"

He looked startled. "I did not say he is dead."

"Ooh!" She let out a gasp. "Do you think I am a moron?" she asked. "Magnus, because Agaba had an accident, that's why the whole village of Umunnero in Lagos left all that they were supposed to be doing on a Monday morning and they are in my compound." She laughed again, a high-pitched laugh.

There is a depth of sorrow that is best left unspoken and untouched. The kind of sorrow that can detach your heart from your soul. Rebecca felt it just then. She left the chair and sat on the floor, her head bowed in sorrow, her body shaking. She broke into an intense sweat even though the weather was cool and not sunny.

"Agaba, ooo!" She let out a wail, beat her chest, got up in a trance-like manner and ran to the gate. They held her. "Who would come to my rescue?" she asked. "Who knows the address of Chukwu? Please take me to Chiokike. Let me ask him, 'Is this how you do?' Who knows where he resides? Tell me where he sits so that I can take my sorrow to him. Give me his address, let me go and wrestle this answer from him. Let me go and ask him where he went on the day that Agaba died. Was he on a journey? Did he perchance go to sleep? But they say he never sleeps and neither slumbers. I'm told he never journeys but I can tell you he went on a journey today."

"Magnus, where is my husband?" She sobbed so bitterly until there was nothing more in her. She felt so hollow, so empty, so light and so heavy at the same time. The women of Umunnero surrounded her and provided her much needed succour.

The burial was another keg of gunpowder. She held her children close and went through the rigours of the funeral. She lost her voice and almost lost her will to live. She had no one now except her aged mother and her children. She was an only child and when she married Agaba she found another home. He was a good man and he made her happy. The demands of the burial were tough; the culture had not changed and the nuances were still almost the same. The Umuada, the daughters of the land, were roving around as usual but she was taciturn, even morose. She observed their slyness and their chameleonic modus operandi and yet gave no words. She knew them and how tough they and their demands could be, but she held herself and avoided them.

Her mother Ijele dealt with them mostly with her co-wives. All that mattered to Rebecca was to bury her husband, do the mourning rituals expected of her and go back to her base Lagos with her children.

Slowly but surely, she felt the change and somehow she accepted and encouraged it. At some point, she was drowning and drifting at the same time. She was shocked at herself and what was happening inside her; a certain kind of nonchalance, anger, sorrow and bereavement at the same time. She began to scoff at Agaba and taunt him. The day they brought back his corpse, she stood at the tailend of his casket and jeered at him.

"So this is what you planned to do to me, eh, Agaba?" Her voice was hoarse from constant crying. "Get up from there if you are a man, but you're not Mbanu, no! You are a coward, that's why you did this." Her first son Onyedi held her tight. He was seventeen, tall and gangly, and had not left his mother's side since their father died.

"It's ok, Mama," he consoled her with tears in his own eyes.

She stared at the remains. Life is not kind, she thought. The only lifeline she had was gone. Her eyes had cried many tears. Her tear ducts were empty. She found herself almost falling apart, but with one look at the faces of her children, she knew she had to be strong, and so she gathered herself and braced herself for the challenges ahead.

They shaved her hair and she wore white. She did not resist them but she was also on the lookout just in case they tried to subject her to any inhumanity in the name of culture and tradition. Her mother Ijele gave her succour at every point. Her father's brother's children and her cousins also came around to console her. She was Ijele's only child and she never expected that this sort of thing would happen to her child. Ijele was in pain but she hid her own so that she could be there to console Rebecca. Ijele was also concerned about traditions, having lost her own husband (Rebecca's father) early in her marriage, a widow herself. But Rebecca told her not to worry about her because she was ready. She was fully prepared for whatever might come up in this period of mourning, the burial of her husband, and subsequently.

So it was that when Magnus crept into her room that night, she trembled with fear at first, then it turned into deep, seething anger. It was so intense that she literally saw flashes of red. She sat up in the dark room where she was kept and braced herself. Even though she was weak from all the burial rituals, a certain kind of strength came into her.

"Who is there?" she asked, though she could clearly see the silhouette of the person through the light coming from the crack in the door.

No answer. The person crept closer and held her tight. Rebecca gave a surly laugh. She was prepared for this and had kept a razor at the tip of her wrapper. Her hand flew there to reassure herself. The razor was solidly lodged.

From the first day of the burial, she had vowed not to accept any indignities. Immediately after Agaba died, the women subtly regaled her with stories of various dimensions and depth on what to expect as a widow. She had listened with her ears wide open whilst her mouth was silent and her eyes bland, devoid of emotions. Her observance of silence was deep and stoic – her mind made up, her resolve unshakeable. She would bear no shame; neither would she submit to any form of oppression or subjugation. Her voice was a little coarse, almost gone from all the crying. She willed herself back to the moment. Magnus had his arms around her, whispering to her in the dark room, but she heard nothing and felt nothing. She was cold.

"Rebecca, this is tradition," Magnus whispered, trying to draw her closer, his breathing rapidly increasing. She could feel his hot breath on her neck. She pushed him off.

"Take your filthy hands off me, you wicked, useless oaf."

He came closer. "If you dare come any closer, I will scream! Magnus, leave my room this minute and go to your wife. Respect the dead, even if you have no vestige of respect inside of you." She stared at him with glaring hate. "Do not let me spit on you. Tradition, my foot! I have no strength in me to fight you, so gently ask yourself out of this room if you don't want disgrace."

"You will regret this, Rebecca; surely you did not just reject me?"

"What are you saying, Magnus?" Rebecca was briefly puzzled. "You actually want to sleep with me on my mourning mat? It is not yet up to six days since your brother Agaba was buried and you want to do this? This is a shame. Don't let me get up from here, Magnus. I will wake up Umunnero, I assure you. The dust on your brother's grave is not yet settled and here you are trying to commit abomination in the name of tradition. Please get out of this place. Do not let me despise you."

He got up and sauntered out of the room angrily.

Magnus did not forget and neither did Rebecca. It was an unspoken happenstance between them. It created a deep gorge between them. Rebecca couldn't have cared less. For her, it was about her dignity – it should not be trampled on, nor should it be taken by force.

Rebecca behaved like it had not happened whilst Magnus carried it about like a scar, a challenge to his manhood.

So when the issue between her daughter Jabo and the pastor happened, he quickly waded in – it was his opportunity to exact revenge, so he took Jabo back to the pastor to spite Rebecca. He told her he was the head of the family and the decision regarding the incident rested with him since she was only a woman.

There are many depths to the soul of a woman and many chambers to her life. Many denials to her, many restrictions, discriminations, abuse – the list is endless. It could never be fully unravelled in a lifetime. Rebecca told me that she had put all her faith in God after she lost Agaba. She spent time in the church when she was not at work. She had three children to raise. She was lonely, yet she had no thoughts of remarrying. The vacuum created by Agaba had to be filled so she gave her all to the church. Being a Christian, she felt that the redemptive power of Jesus Christ was all she needed to wade through life. She never questioned the 'prophet', her man of God. Whatever he said, she did without questioning. She elevated him to the status of a god.

On the day she told her story, her eyes were red and her body trembled. Her regrets were on full display, but who knows how often this life will betray one? Who knows how human beings in our presentation of ourselves can become destructive to one another? The manipulations welded through religion and religious apparatus are mind-boggling and pervasive.

Amadio, my dear friend! How can you call and sound concerned, even benevolent? Sometimes when you speak in whispers and when you ask of others and the situation in 'our' country, I feel like you're mocking me. I hear your accent has changed. 'Hahaha, oh dear me.' Today is not one of the days when I try to assuage your curiosity. It is not one of the days when I try to indulge your flights of fantasy.

On the day Jabo was raped by the prophet, Rebecca took her for night vigil. After the prayers, the prophet asked Rebecca to let Jabo stay for further prayers. He said Jabo needed to be prayed for, but he was not sure why the 'Spirit' was telling him and 'putting it in his mind'. But it had to be done to take away the dark clouds hovering over her, otherwise she would encounter difficulties in future, he said. The prophet daddy had spoken and Rebecca could not challenge him. His words were, 'Yea' and 'Amen'. What he says, Rebecca must do as an obedient follower. Daddy must be obeyed. Nothing more, nothing less.

Rebecca curtsied before the altar and left. Jabo was uneasy because, according to Rebecca, she was a budding ten-year-old child. She felt she did not want to be left alone and wanted to go with her mother. She was always with Rebecca and never left her side except when she had to go to school. But this was a spiritual situation, Rebecca reasoned, and she needed prayers. She convinced her to stay so that 'Daddy', the prophet, could pray for her. Rebecca had asked the prophet if she could stay whilst the prayer lasted, but the prophet told her it was not necessary since the prayers would take long and she had work to do. He promised that she would be returned to her in the morning. So Rebecca left her child in the hands of a wolf all in the name of prayers and her conviction that he was a man of God.

Some kinds of remembrance of events tend towards fresh torture and heartbreak. 'Confront your fears,' they say. Some memories need not be unearthed, I say. Rebecca blew her nose, her eyes fiery red as she recollected the incident.

"Jabo said that he led her into his inner chambers, laid hands on her head, anointed her head with olive oil and sprayed holy water on her. Laid her out on the bed in his inner chamber and defiled her. Whilst he was at it, he stuffed her mouth with cloth even as she screamed at the searing pain between her thighs."

This was the beginning of evil against another human being, a girl child that could have been his grandchild. This is also the fate of so many girl children out there. Many will suffer in silence. For so many, their families will take them through the path of shame. All their lives, they'll bear the scars of this violation, this violence and its shame. Some will die, whilst some may never truly heal or recover. He told her it was a holy ordinance and that she was sacred and a special vessel to be used by God. This was the first time Rebecca could sit and tell the story. She was still in regret. She has still not forgiven herself. She shook as she told the story and she wept bitterly. She felt she had betrayed her daughter and her late husband to think that her child's life was destroyed in her quest to quench the pains brought on by the death of her husband.

After the death of Agaba, she had sought solace in the church more than ever before; she became committed. The same place she sought refuge and solace became her albatross. She told me that the pangs of the pain of guilt often overtook her, especially in her solemn and sober moments. That every time she remembered Agaba or visited his grave, there's a faint reminder of failure tugging at her chest. When Agaba was alive, he held the church in suspicion, especially the new churches and their new ways. Agaba often would wonder at women and how they were held spellbound by these pastors, their men of God. He would often tell Rebecca to go alone since he did not want to be hoodwinked. Agaba was a protestant by birth and chose to remain so. He said he was baptised in the Anglican Church and that is what he knew. Pentecostalism did not appeal to him; they came with complicated ways and teachings, and he would have none of it. Rebecca would often invite him for 'programs' in her new church, but he would decline attending so that he would not be deceived.

Now the burden of guilt rested so heavily on Rebecca's shoulders knowing that her husband would have questioned her carelessness in the face of this. Her husband would have sent any person who dared to do this kind of evil, repulsive thing to his daughter to an early grave. Her mourning became double; the loss of her husband and the loss of Jabo's innocence. Then the mockery of Magnus and his handling of Jabo's rape by the pastor. It was time to take his pound of flesh since the burial of Agaba. He placed the entire blame on Rebecca and insisted on the pastor taking Jabo since he had defiled her. Magnus insisted the pastor must pay for the damages done to Jabo. It felt transactional to Rebecca. She thought the pastor should have been arrested. Magnus refused, accusing her of all manner of things, including sleeping with the 'prophet'.

He came with their town's people and took the child by force to the pastor, asking that he make amends or face serious consequences. He accused Rebecca of having an affair with the prophet in front of their neighbours. Rebecca replied neither to him nor his co-conspirators. She kept quiet and went about her business in pain, biding for the right time and patiently waiting for him to finish taking his pound of flesh. He was angry that Rebecca denied him access to her flesh. He was smarting from making a fool of himself! No one knew what the issue was between him and Rebecca. This was the time to show his manliness.

Rebecca said that she found virtue in silence. She said she found virtue in perseverance and knew that she had to wait. After Magnus had finished exacting his vengeance by humiliating her before their townspeople and accusing her of all sorts of immorality, he still was not pacified. The silent war he had with Rebecca was still on. He refused to be appeased. Magnus continued to accuse Rebecca of knowingly handing over her child to the man to be defiled. The prophet denied touching Jabo; he said he did not understand what they were saying. He claimed he asked one of the 'workers' in church to take Jabo back to Rebecca after the overnight deliverance. Even when the man of God denied touching Jabo and defiling her, Rebecca kept quiet and would not immediately join issues with the prophet. But she told me that the power she had over them was the fact that Jabo was her child and she would not be alive to see anybody ruin her.

The day she went to the church to take back her child, Rebecca went with her brothers and her cousins from her father's side. When she got to the church, she stood in the middle of the auditorium and called the pastor to bring her child to her. Rebecca shouted his full name and declared in that auditorium what he had done to her child. There were people who had come to receive prayers and they asked her to respect the church of God and the man of God. They tried to force her out; they knew her and knew her story but their prophet had told them not to believe her. She had become an anathema to the church, an outcast, a dissident. She stood her ground with her head held high, tears streaming down her face whilst her brothers waited outside and called on the man of God again, declaring his sins against her child before the altar.

Tears flowed freely but there was no going back. Here she was, speaking on behalf of her child's innocence, crying out against evil and wickedness. Declaring war against violent exploitation and access to her child's body. She was not going to back down. The weight of her child's stolen innocence was on her shoulders and the pain of the so-called man of God's deception laid like hot lead on her heart. She trembled slightly as she stood before the altar, which she thought was smeared with the offerings of her daughter's desecration. Her whole body was full of fight as she stood there waiting to see Jabo and take her home. She remembered the first time she came to the church, how Agaba warned her to be careful, and she sighed in regret.

Rebecca could not wait to see the prophet to tell him his abominations. She was in torment, her heart torn to shreds and heavy.

The man of God crept from his office and asked his workers to take the child back to Rebecca. When Jabo saw her, she flew into her arms. Jabo had been there for forty-eight hours. Magnus was still mounting pressure on the prophet, according to what Rebecca heard. She couldn't care less. She was not comfortable with his way of handling the situation. Her child must not spend one more second in this place! Standing in front of the pew, Rebecca told the prophet that he had committed an abomination and shed the blood of her child. She told him that she would take back her child but would not pretend that nothing had happened. She told him that it was war between her and him till eternity. She would continue to cry to God to remember that she was a widow that had had her rights trampled upon and her child's innocence stolen, her soul and chastity tainted, lies told against her and her child. Rebecca told him that she would continue to pray to God to remember his sins against her. She said she was not ready to forgive.

The people that came to receive prayers stood as if nothing was happening, but there was complete silence. The prophet stood by the side of the altar with half-closed eyes and swayed from side to side, saying nothing, waiting for her to go so that he could start the midweek service. She was now an outcast and he had no business with her. She was no longer one of the faithful. She was a rebel and had been blacklisted for having the audacity to challenge the prophet. No member of the church should be in contact with her. It was an order which, once truncated, made one an outcast.

Rebecca walked with her head held high, tears streaming down her face, snot on her nose, and stood in front of the prophet. People stared in shock wondering what she would do next. She opened her mouth and spat at the feet of the prophet. She raised her voice and said to him, 'From today, Earth will reject you and heaven will also reject you for the evil you have done to my child.' She took the hands of Jabo, who was somewhat calm through it all, and walked out of the church. She cried so bitterly and refused to be consoled. As the evening rays fixed their gaze on the earth, it was unimaginable what sights they beheld regarding the behaviour of the children of men. Days later, the church was burnt down by some 'unidentified' young men in the area, they say, who insisted on avenging the wrong done to Jabo. They said that the man of God was in the habit of raping young girls and nothing was done by the elders in the community. They took the law into their own hands and razed down the church. The prophet fled the area. His 'faithful' scattered. The street had spoken.

Life itself has a whole lot of complexities. This is why I would say to you to be happy always. Do your best. When you trust, leave room for evaluations; do not jump into trust with both feet. Do well to test the water first. And sometimes welcome melancholy so that your soul can be sober and cleansed. Do not imagine life; just live life. Let life guide you through its often winding paths. As you go, remember to free your spirit. Allow silence in your chambers sometimes. Remove the noise and find a place where you can stay and receive yourself back. For the days when you do not recognise yourself, look at your feet and be thankful for your journey. Rid yourself of unpleasantness by observing the sun on a cloudy day. Close your eyes sometimes and sit in the sun and get soaked by its rays. You must do well to find peace in the midst of chaos. Find time to smile and time also to love yourself. Life will always turn up surprises. To place the weight of the world on your shoulders and carry it on your head is not wisdom. When you do not have answers, go to sleep. It will become clearer when you wake and the answers will come to you. Our scars, our imperfections, are ours to bear. They show how well we have done with life's battles, how well we have taken our lessons and how much we have learnt.

Rebecca remained thankful that her child, her only girl child, was back with her. When things spin out of your control, have the temerity to stop your soul from worrying. Is it possible to be silent or sit still in the face of a raging war? On the day that your boat is capsizing, is it possible to look up and have faith and not be flustered? I do not know the answers but I love the feel of the questions. Why do I lose my mind over the small things and why do I lose my life over the seemingly big things? These too shall pass. Now as I lay down in my chambers on my bed with sleep hovering over my entire being, I think about Rebecca but my mind rests on Nda. The tale of two different kinds of strength. The mysteriousness of reactions to events and how strangely men accord different interpretations to life's sudden happenstances, tragedies and joy.

I do not understand how Nda could take all these in her stride without as much as a conversation with the man that killed her child. I do not understand how she continues to step into the same church that had the evil perpetrator of this crime against her child still in charge. How does she stick out her tongue and her hand to receive Holy Communion and prayers still with this man? How? What sort of religion is this? Some days I wonder truthfully if I can easily say that I understood this woman. This person, my friend Nda. She often told me that when life presents itself, she has a way of bypassing its pains and numbing them out. It helps her float and rise beyond the grief so that sometimes she does not remember what has happened, how it happened and how it hit her.

She said it has helped save her life, numbing out her pains.

I was confused by her submission because I have often seen her cry. I have seen her rushed to the hospital because of high blood pressure. I have seen her burst out in anger unnecessarily because of the lack of confrontation of issues she hid from.

I don't think it saved her. I think it buried her and she stopped living. But then these are my assumptions and my own observations from where I am sitting. Nda has moved on pretty well. Her life is fully engrossed in raising Chukwubife and she is doing it beautifully well. So maybe I'm wrong? Just maybe.

Nda told me that she often rushes towards forgiveness and

offers it quickly to her offenders so that she can reclaim her life and her peace to ultimately move on from the issues of life faster. She doesn't like to dwell on issues. There was no need for that, she said. So why is your blood pressure high? I asked. But I met a stonewalled response as usual, which is the case whenever my curiosity touches on her deep-earthed nerves. I'm often stonewalled because of my observations. Obliterating her reality hits home and times when she doesn't want to face the truth. Always in denial. Always!She told me that when her husband Bernard left her, she nearly died. She had built her life around him and her self-worth. And so, when he walked away from her because she could not bear him more children, especially male children, she lost her mind temporarily and could not remember things for some time. She told me she battled with this lack of remembrance of things and events for three long years after he left her, and her child Eka suffered too. When she regained herself, she vowed not to put things deeply in her mind no matter what that was and from whom the offence was coming. Nda told me that the church helped her in regaining herself. Maybe the prophet also. Still, I do not understand why the man of God, her man of God, is walking free without so much as a 'why' from her. Nda forbade me to talk about him with her. It was none of my business, she said. So this is my cross to bear, a puzzle for the rest of my life.

My mind went back to Bernard's treatment of her. He practically abandoned her and Eka their child and never looked back. I thought to myself, this was violence of another kind. It was both a traumatic experience for Nda and for Eka.

But Nda had sat on it and made her emotions null and void. That you made a vow with a man and he left you just because you were not able to give him a male child is violence.

The time you made the promise to the woman, married her, held her hands and went to the altar with her, you should have recanted your selfishness. That's what I thought. That's what I strongly believe, both on the side of a man and on the side of a woman. Recant your selfishness and bring your sacrifice and commitment home. You should have known that the journey would amount to its own twists and turns.

Biologically, it was Bernard her husband who owed her that male seed, not the other way round. This is violence, Nda. A deliberate kind of humiliation. The insincere act of giving a dog a bad name just to hang it. As far as I'm concerned, for him to have left you without so much as looking back all these years, nor asking after his child Eka, is violence of a certain kind. But as usual, Nda, your feelings were submerged, I've observed. I'm absolutely sure you are living in denial. It's also ridiculous to me that Nda still has her wedding band on her finger. She is living with this kind of strange hope that one day the prodigal son will come back.

I feel like no man, or woman especially, should be made to go through emotional torture and there are certain kinds of torment one should bravely resist and shun. This kind of betrayal of trust and love is violence unequalled, as far as I am concerned. Nda does not deserve this sort of treatment, nor does any human being at that. Sometimes we allow toxic, negative situations to bury us instead of standing up to them and walking away. We are concerned about what people will say. What society will say and how society will see us, the barrage of condemnation that will follow if we leave a toxic, negative relationship, especially marriage and especially as women. We do not ask ourselves, 'What about my life? Am I truly living? Or am I dying or dead already inside?' No one really cares. People have their own baggage tied around their necks. We should instead concentrate on how to salvage our own soul and lives from the clutches of the toxic, selfish person who obviously never cared from the onset or whose feelings have changed.

I believe that everyone should hold their own firmly in any relationship, be able to tell the truth to the other party and not entertain violence nor deceit of any kind. Sometimes one should shun certain kinds of weakness in the name of conceding for peace to reign. There are times of concessions to truth and there are times of forgiveness of infractions, but nobody should continue to accept toxic behaviour from anybody in the name of keeping a relationship. Know the boundaries. Keep the flag of respect and recognise the deal-breaker. Love is never enough; there is accountability, compassion, empathy, faithfulness, forgiveness and truth. There are others, but can we earnestly put these in practice?

I'm puzzled by certain kinds of unionism, the coming together of the mismatched, misfits, rebels, the uncouth and the likes, but I'm incredulous in the face of narcissism as a match. Nothing good can ever come out of it. Then there are the co-travellers, the people who come together for business interests, the marauders, those that steal relationships and make vows with the gullible and the naive. Then the wanderers, those hit by wanderlust that have lots of cravings and shavings by the side. Also the liars. I'm mortified by those that lead others to their deaths and yet they wonder why I am not married. The world is such a place.

Nda is a wonder in a human body but life happened to her. I still marvel at how she has been able to surmount her life's challenges with incredible grace. I see the scars come out sometimes, often in the evening when warmth and comfort are needed, yet she abides in a certain cocoon of contentment without complaint. And when the dark days hit her occasionally, she holds her expectations submerged in a place of cobwebs where she does not allow them to come out nor allow them to ask for anything. This is where my confusion lies, for one should be able to let it out sometimes. Any time I ask if she will remarry, she will look at me in a dark way and ask if I do not see her wedding band. Case closed. Matters adjourned indefinitely.

What more can I say?

Rebecca said she found strength in her resolve to face her issues, to acknowledge where she had failed her child. Her carelessness and partial weakness in the face of culture and the judgment of people.

She said to me the pot is not completely broken; it has cracks in it but I have a war chest of love to bring healing to my child, and as long as there is life and God is in heaven, my child will heal. Jabo will be alright, she said, and the cracks will fade away eventually even if the brokenness remains.

For, ultimately, she agreed that there will always be wounds, but her job, she said to me, is not to allow them to fester. 'By the strength of my love, my child will regain her life and even though they meant it for evil, God will turn it around for good,' she said. I could see the hope in her eyes and yet the tears were still there. She was still on the road to recovery one day at a time. I am still intrigued by her attitude to the church and religion.

When I brought it up again, she sighed. 'I am not fighting them. My not stepping into a church again is to avoid being a conduit for their evil.' With raised eyebrows I stared at her, startled, because this is not commonplace amongst our people. This was a strange observation. Religion is everything to our people, a kind of salve. We often mindlessly sell ourselves to the men of the cloth, to their holy oils, their holy water, their incense and their abracadabra. You are told emphatically not to judge and, depending on the circle where you find yourself, you are told to keep your opinions to yourself. You are warned to respect the man of God, the prophet and their likes. 'Touch not my anointed and do my prophet no harm' is their mantra. To hear this from Rebecca was a certain form of reawakening and satisfaction that she had her reasoning cap on. She waved aside my surprise and continued. 'I do not want to be a mercenary in their hands. A conductor and conduit for evil behaviour. A merchant of falsehood.' I wonder why they keep merchandising the name of God for their selfish reasons? God should never be used as a means to an end. There is no difference between these merchants of the gospel who are actually businessmen and our politicians. We were still looking at them thinking that the church in Nigeria had brought hope to soothe and take away the pains inflicted on us by our politicians and the new democracy. Whilst we were still looking at them like salve to our wounds, like balm to our pain, something grave fell on us. Men became interpreters for God. They became citadels of confusion unto themselves and their listeners. They became slimy, they became thieves. The robbery of people's lives and their resources became their daily mandate.

"Ifedi, there are days I wished to die because of what had happened to my child, but one look at her face, just one look at her face, I knew I had to be alive to fight for her life. Jabo, my child, must be fully restored and reinstituted. That is my job. Rape is a repulsive thing. A deep darkness. A malevolent depravity. Violence belying putrefaction. A certain kind of degeneration of the mind. There are no words nor adjectives to aptly qualify it and those that engage in it.

Agaba would have loved me to be alive to raise our children, so that is what I have resolved to do. Regardless of who helps me or who throws pain at me, I will continue to rise up daily and fight for my life and that of my children.

Jabo may be broken, but that broken pot is in the process of being mended. We will turn this pain into triumph and lessons and that is it for me.

"Ifedi, life must continue and the music must go on. Yes, often times I wake to chills in the middle of the night and I'm startled by my carelessness. It seems strange to me that this happened in a moment of careless, blind trust; a slip. And in the time when I was most vulnerable. But I accept all of my weaknesses and that moment of bad judgment. I accept that I was careless but I must continue to live my life regardless.

The frustration of a man is constantly ticking, whether by his actions or inaction, or his environment.

"You see, Ifedi, my dear, there comes a time in the life of a man, any man, when one should seek peace and clarity. It takes a lot more to find peace and forgiveness with oneself. It takes a lot to find clarity, but the journey must continue and the show must go on. Like a mother hen with her chicks, that is the way I have gathered my children under my arms away from prying eyes, away from wicked men, away from the church and men of the cloth. Life is complex, my sister. When you think that, your troubles are over. Wait for it, you're up against another tornado, another upsurge of violence against your being. 'What does not kill a man can only make him stronger.'"You see, I'm on the street of healing and that is where I have taken my child to. I am glad she is comforted. Some days she cries in the middle of the night, not understanding the sudden violent initiation into adulthood, but I am always close by to wipe her tears and reassure her. If you want to know how far you have come in life and how rough it has been, just look at your feet; it will help you appreciate your life more, find hope and peace as you journey."

Rebecca's triumph was the reclaiming of her child. "Nwanyibuife," I sighed, meaning 'a woman is valuable'. Indeed, a woman is a human being of value and should be treated as such. I look at Rebecca and Nda now and can only draw inspiration of hope, tenacity, patience and endurance. Chukwubife brought redemption to Nda whilst Jabo brought another type of redeeming power and triumph over evil to Rebecca. Life must continue. We must fight for life. We must continue to live and embrace hope. Make sure you live and not merely exist. I urge you to live.

Amadio! My day has come. As I look at this place, there's no melancholy. I cleared my desk, cleared my drawers and shut down my system. I removed my ID card from my neck with my name Ifedinma Obiakor written boldly on it. I love my name. I've had the ID card with its black cord on my neck for twelve years. Sometimes changing the rope and the plastic holder. It assures my entrance into the building every morning. Like a ritual, I would place it on my neck daily with my smiling picture beaming from its plastic mould. As I took it off my neck, I felt relieved. It seemed as if there was a cutting of an invisible umbilical cord. I felt free. As I heard the click of the system and the Microsoft signature shutting down sound, I felt the euphoria of freedom. This place does not serve me anymore.

We have limited time to be on Earth; we should make the most of it. Here I am making haste to redeem my time here. For some time, I did not know what it was nor the shape it would take. Now I know. My life should be lived in the service of others. This job was not one of them. I took a last look at the environment; I felt no nostalgia. I was leaving behind a monstrous manager, a man who never wanted to hear the truth nor own it. But it was not all doom and gloom; I was fortunate to have worked with four pleasant zonal heads who were thoughtful and kind and provided great leadership. In fact, this manager I was leaving was a half-baked, semi-illiterate man when it came to education and the study of life, who had manipulated his way through the system to get to where he was. He often boasted about how he, a son of nobody, was now 'a big man' and how he had the power to sack anybody as he liked since he was the branch manager! I often wondered how he got into the system, but his likes were scattered all over, a testament of a country in dire straits and in dire need of serious development.

I left a system and an establishment that was in desperate need of revamping because I saw a weak centre and a saturated top. A system foisted in the malady of archaic, strangulating methods of leadership which was in dire need of truth — a new attitude with absolute change in its processes and in its leadership dynamics and culture. This was a whitewash, often not keeping its words. There was the silence that was expected in the face of oppression and I would have none of it. A certain masking of the very truth, a denial of clarity and the stagnation of your very life if you dared stay on. Then the excuse of no jobs if I wished to listen and stay on. Well yes, there are no white-collar jobs readily available because there is no government and no enabling environment, but there are the blue-collar, the yellow, then brown, and all sorts of jobs out there. If I will myself to see it, life is all about choices. You get to choose. But Ifedinma, it was not your place to tell them, neither was it your place to remind them, I told myself.

Often times, the leadership presented itself in arrogance and would wield overwhelming power over its subjects. Sorry, staff! I should bite my itinerant tongue. Subjects who were afraid of the murky economic quagmire of Nigeria, my country, and therefore reacted cowardly in the face of suppression, oppression, subjugation and abuse of leadership power through its ranks. Staff who could not question processes that negated human dignity and respect. It was a viral load as they were oppressed, overtly and covertly, and it also trickled down to the foot soldiers. I packed my bags and without so much as a goodbye exited silently the way I entered, thankful still for the opportunity of experience in a financial environment. Thankful for the experience of a job in a country where the majority of university graduates are roaming the streets without jobs, without an iota of hope.

The HR exit interview was quick, brisk and brief. I was still grateful that I got this job almost immediately after my university education, but it was a job in an industry I did not quite like. I sat for the exams, passed and got the role. Now as I exited to pursue my real purpose, there were no regrets except that I should have left earlier. It was at the last interview with HR that I felt a little emotional as I took a final look at the organisation where I had put in work for more than a decade. I still had a lot of admiration for this place in a certain way – an ironic observation. I am still amazed at its braggadocio and its ability to hold its staff in a clasp with flimsy excuses. I am amazed at its tongue-twisting lies and the way it has bestowed on its staff the euphoria and illusions of greatness and of being a great place to work. The mysterious, cunning ways it has glazed their eyes with curtains of the more you look, the less you see. Unfulfilled promises beckon my mind and beg for my remembrance, even though it had become a toxic and negative environment for me.

As I left this place, I was not going to miss it but I had loads of lessons in my kitty. I had some seriously shocking lessons in human behaviour and how conflicting and complex it can be. I had some surprising lessons in doublespeak and the mafia-like associations within this place. I experienced first-hand what it meant to sit at the table of liars and the scornful, to be judged and stripped of your humanity. What triumphed in the end was my ability to walk away from a system that no longer served me, one which I did not want to be associated with anymore.

Goodbyes can be hard sometimes. It depends on who is saying it, who is receiving it, the reason for saying it, where you're saying it and the occasion. It's never easy but then life goes on.

So long. Hello, new day. Hello, tomorrow. I feel the freshness of a new start. I close my eyes and open my heart and my soul to this fresh start. Daunting, scary, but I feel free, very free. It's an unknown path, the road less travelled, but I embrace it with all my heart. Every life is a story unravelling. Every life is a journey in choices, seasons and stages. Some choose to live bravely, others out of breath, some others below the radar. The way you chose is the way you journey. Your understanding of life, yours and yours alone. The validation of you and who you are or what you become is subject to your own interpretation. How you survive is how many of your flanks you left to the wild, how many you protected, and how many you allowed enemy war tanks to pass through. Your euphoria of joy yours and yours alone. You must hold yourself accountable, for naked we came into this world and naked we must return. Some days are yo-yo-like, others fraught with despair. Some days just don't make sense at all. As I walked down the hallways of this place, I wondered at people and our different reactions to the issues of life.

When I told Mma Eka that I was quitting, she thought I was mad.

"Ifedinma, you're a strange one. This same job people are clamouring for, killing themselves to have, is the same you're leaving to go and pick up the chalk. The spirit that reincarnated you is stubborn, strong and strange. I hope it is not a malevolent spirit.

This spirit should also at least be kind to you."

I laughed. As I made to reply, she held up her hand.

"What can I do or say to stop you? Nobody can ever stop you. But your chi, your personal god, is a kind one because you always succeed even where you're expected to fail.

So if I say do not quit, I'm wasting my time because you only hear the drumbeat of your own mind and soul. The only sorrow now is that you're going away from this city and I may not see you often."

There was a long silence between us. My heart was also heavy at the uncertainty of this journey but my countenance did not show it. It was not an easy decision and it may not be an easy journey, but it was one that brought me enormous relief and peace. Then I broke the silence.

"Nda, you remain in my heart, and as often as possible I will come and see you." I tried to reassure her. It was an assurance that was not necessary because I knew I would always return to this place.

"Why don't you get married, eh, Ifedinma?" she asked

suddenly.

I raised my eyebrows and looked at her quizzically. She took my hands in a conciliatory manner and smiled tenderly – this, my awesome, beautiful friend who never gives up on me, who will always, always want the best for me. Always in my corner, loving, cheering and rooting for me. She has been through so much yet always looks out for others even in the midst of her pain.

Slowly she spoke and tried to convince me, as she often would, in a gentle manner.

"I have tried to move you out of fear into a place of expectancy, expectancy for the best outcomes in marriage, yet you sneer and snort at marriage as if you enjoy being lonely. How strange it is that a young, full-bodied lady like you would often dismiss marriage with a wave of the hand. Why do you continue to hold tenaciously to singlehood even at this age?" She looked at me questioningly.

"Must one be married as a woman to be fulfilled?" I asked. "Must we always have this conversation of ticking time and menopause around women?"

"Ha! Ifedi Nwannem, it is not good for a woman to be alone and unmarried at your age. Without a husband, without children," she said.

"But it's good for a man to be alone without pressure mounting on him nor time ticking?" I inquired with a scoff.

"There you go again. I'm not here to argue with you," she continued, almost frustrated. "All I'm asking you is to get married and have children like every other right-thinking woman. Like your mates," she pleaded.

"Oooh, Nda, like my mates, like any other right-thinking woman, you say? What if I'm not happy?" I almost screamed. "What if I don't even feel presently like getting married? Why the pressure? Why should my fertility be questioned because at this point and stage of my life I simply do not feel like getting married or being in a committed relationship? Why are women conditioned towards marriage and childbearing? All our lives it seems like the goal is simply to marry and have children, even in this 21st century.

Why?" I asked, looking at her with my eyebrows raised.

"So it boils down to conditioning now?" she asked, looking at me disapprovingly.

"Well, yes," I answered.

"I don't know why the sum total of a woman's life will continue to lean towards whether she's married or not. Whether she's able to remain in the marriage come rain, come sunshine, through physical, emotional and psychological trauma or whether she divorces.

"I'm always petrified at your nonchalance and your defence whenever this subject is raised. I often wonder if there is something you're hiding. Something you don't want me to know," she replied.

"That's ridiculous coming from you, Nda," I said, laughing. "You of all people should not think like that."

"Then imagine what other people might be thinking," she said.

"I am not bothered about other people. I am bothered about me and that is enough.""Ifedinma, get married, that is all!"

"I still don't think marriage is for me with what I see around me," I replied.

"Suit yourself, Ifedinma. This is not right. You don't stop your life based on other people's experiences; rather, you learn from it and improve on your life based on what you've learnt from their supposed mistakes," she said.

"What is not right, Nda?" I asked but she ignored me.

"Nda, your husband left you abruptly after ten years of marriage because of your inability to give him a male child even in this 21st century. That is what is not right and it is ridiculous.

Yet you don't find it ridiculous and neither have you ever questioned the fact that he promised you forever, promised to be by your side eternally and then left you in a ditch. That is what is not right and not my not getting married." She sighed and looked away.

"So what changed? What changed in your relationship? That is the question that begs for answers and that is where my own difficulties in the understanding and interpretation of marriage lie," I continued to push. "Why was he not bold enough to tell you to your face that it was because he wanted a male child to validate his maleness and his manhood? What changed, Nda? But, as usual, you will plead the 'fifth right'? You never want to ever talk about it." I was angry. I felt she was blind-sided or pretending to be so.

"See, as long as people are not careful to commit diligently and truthfully to someone and be healthy in their behaviour towards each other in marriage, then count me out."

"Ifedinma, your life should not stop because of other

people's malady in marriage," she said slowly. "Your life should not end because of fears. Yes, Bernard and I did not work out, and yet my life did not end because of it." "But your pillows taste salty because of sultry, windy, rain-soaked nights when you keep awake to mourn what should have been and cry out your eyes for how he promised you earth and gave you wind," I said forcefully, still vibrating with anger at this sort of treatment.

Nda continued in a calm voice as only she knew how to do in the face of irritation and even provocation. "Ifedi Nwannem! Forget Bernard and me. Don't take Panadol for another man's headache," she said with finality dripping in her voice. "Don't dance in my shame." She raised her voice slightly. "Allow me to stand in it but not wallow in it. It is not the definition of me, nor will I ever allow myself to wallow in its obscure, elusive nature. Shame!" she called out, gesticulating with her hands. "I refuse to be a tool in your hand, shame! Neither will I ever throw a pity party for you nor for myself," she said, slightly sitting up in her chair.

"There were nights I did not believe I would see the morning because of pain and heartbreak. Days my breath left me. Sometimes the afternoons did not come quick in my own estimation because I was in limbo. Bernard thought I was a mockery but here I am, still living. He erected an emblem of shame in my place but I am still standing. Surviving the unimaginable, the death of my only child Eka! No one can ever know the depth of my suffering, my fears and my tears. Not even you, Ifedi, with the depth of our closeness and friendship. I hid it from you, Ifedinma, because of its fiery, caustic nature, this pain that I have hidden in my soul. I did not want anybody to suffer alongside me. Not Eka nor anyone at all. I am still alive and well, trudging on. Not forgotten by the Almighty God. You think Bernard won? No, he didn't. No victor! No vanquished," she declared. "Just misplaced priorities and chasing of shadows by a man who was not brave enough to face life in truth!"

I laughed wryly. I was enjoying this. This was the first time I could get her to talk about her marriage. It had been a blind spot and she had never wanted to discuss it.

"Nda, stop hiding behind the curtains, please!" I goaded her, wanting her to talk more. But she looked at me and kept quiet. "Come out plain and agree with me."

"Agree on what?" she retorted, temporarily irritated. Then she recoiled, sensing my bait.

"That society should stop the blackmail of women. The conditioning, the grooming and the suggestions that life for a woman should only end in marriage and childbirth," I continued.

"A woman should be heard, seen, felt and not muted. She should never be an afterthought. There should not be any surprises or any attempt at being surprised when she wins or when she's winning. There should not be sombre looks at her when she's assertive and demanding of her rights.

She should not be reminded that she's a woman and she should never be reduced to just a 'thing'. A flight of fancy. It is a loss to society to continue to treat women this way. A very heavy loss."

Nda looked at me in an observatory manner and said

nothing. To her, I was a recalcitrant child. A rebel of a sort. So I continued.

"In the scheme of things and looking at creation through the eyes of the creator, he made woman and womanhood beautiful. The crafting, the moulding and the process of this creation, incredible. It's seen in the beauty of her eyes, the swaying of her hips and the velvety smoothness of her skin. But these are just physical attributes. Nda, the spirituality of becoming a woman is deep, so deep it should not be trifled with.

I guess the world is afraid to experience the fullness of the manifestations of woman. Therefore, it's easy to trample on her and cage her in order to reduce and obliterate her rights and the comeliness of her intelligence and the redemption she can bring if she's allowed equal space and equal platforms with men."

"It's not about equality. Don't I know all this, Ifedinma?" she said in exasperation. "Who is talking about equality? I totally agree with you in some aspects, but not in the totality of your hard stance, let this be known to you." I watched her from where I was sitting expressionless.

"I vehemently disagree with some of your positions," she continued. "We have our culture but let's not get into it now because we have our areas of disagreement in this regard. But I'm asking that you get married, give a man a chance in your life. That's what I am asking of you right now. That is my concern. What are you doing, being single at this age?" she asked.

"I'm discovering myself, Nda. That's what I'm doing, since

you can't hear me. I've seen people destroyed by this same marriage," I answered quickly, clicking my tongue.

"And I've seen and known beautiful marriages that produced beautiful children and gave beautiful hope to the future," she replied. "Ifedinma, give marriage a chance, biko!"

"I know that I cannot convince you to leave well enough alone, Nda, but you have to realise that I'm not against the institution of marriage. I'm against the hypocrisies and selfishness of the people who engage in it. I do not understand how a hot hearth becomes cold soon after it is stirred. Then the loathing of each other, the hate, the lies and the eventual dissolution of marriage contracted with 'great love'.""It takes courage to build a marriage. Tenacity, wisdom, patience, perseverance, love, commitment, humility and selflessness," she replied.

"And yet Bernard left?" I asked sarcastically.

She shrugged. "It was his choice to leave, not mine." She continued in that voice that said, 'I'm over it but not so sure'. "I'm confused but clear about my own intentions. More so, I'm not hating him and I'm not judging him. I just wish him well. You cannot determine what anybody really wants, you cannot determine what keeps anybody happy nor what keeps them awake at night," she said.

"I'm puzzled that your love, commitment, sincerity and hard work couldn't keep him," I said loosely.

"The question now would be, is he still happy?" she said with her eyes half-closed. "In the midst of all these things, Ifedinma, I'm still happy and grateful to be here. I'm grateful in a very surprising way because I've accepted within me that

Bernard is not the sum total of my life. It took a long time, I must say, but the moment I realised that, I took back my life and regained myself. He ceased to have power over me a very long time ago."

"So why are you still putting on your wedding band?" I asked, "Why? If indeed he has no power over you."

She looked at me and smiled in a very confusing, befuddled way, then she answered smoothly, "I took a vow, Ifedi, that's why I still wear my band."

"Really?" I replied. "It is not enough explanation for someone who never looked back since he left. No contact, no nothing. This is the throwing of loyalty to the dogs, believe me! I believe that deep down in your soul is the thinking that he may one day come back," I said.

"Well maybe," she answered. "Who knows? But I don't think I am waiting for him. I wear my wedding band out of habit," she said flatly.

"This is strange, to say the least, very strange," I said.

"I realised that I'm ok being by myself," she continued. "At first I was angry. Angry at myself for the choices I made. Angry that I allowed someone so much power over me. I tried my best, Ifedi. I really, really tried. I went out of my way to be the best wife, the best woman and the best housekeeper, totally supportive of Bernard. But it did not work. He wanted other things. After I had Eka, it was difficult for me to conceive again. Then began my visit to different spiritual places. Hospital to hospital. Some places are too horrid to mention. I felt I had failed myself, failed him and failed everyone else." She looked at me with glazed eyes and shook her head.

"I took one dangerous journey to visit a woman at Awka near Ebenebe, a known witch doctor, in search of more children to satisfy him. It was a night journey for cleansing and I had a bath at one river deep in the middle of the night. In the middle of nowhere. There was nobody on our way to the river and I had a calabash on my head. It was just me, the woman and her apprentice. Yet I was a Christian. You could hear the night owls and deep, eerie silence. It was after that journey that I decided that Eka was enough. Before I left for that journey, he showed no concern.

"When I came back, all hell let loose. Bernard became another thing altogether. A stranger. You know how it is with our people once there are infertility issues or delay in childbearing. The woman takes the full blame and must seek a solution to remedy the situation, even when the reverse might be the case. You receive solicited and unsolicited advice. One night after we had quarrelled, Bernard and I, he told me that I had failed as a woman for not giving him a male child. He said to me, 'Look around you, you have only one child after ten years of marriage and no son'. He was so cruel that night, Ifedi Nwannem, and he thoroughly despised me. Bernard said some horrible things I dare not say to another person. As I curled up at the corner of our room with the duvet over my head, I also knew that I had it. I decided then that whether he stayed or left belonged to him, it was a decision he alone would have to make.

I mourned our marriage but I had no regrets. I had married, I had a child and it was enough. So, Ifedi, when he decided to call it quits and left, I had no guilt and I released him. As I sit here, there is still no separation between us, no divorce. I feel like someone whose husband has been on a long journey. I still care very much for him, if I dare say so."

I looked at my friend in wonderment as I wanted to say that she was contradicting herself. That indeed she had corroborated my suspicions finally, that she was still waiting for Bernard as I suspected. That she needed to heal and move on in the real sense of it, but it seemed as if a force had clamped my mouth shut and I just stared at her.

"Ifedi," she continued, "marriage is for the brave, the courageous and fools. Your commitment to it should be selfless and watertight. I sent words to him when our child died. I got no words back."

I shuddered at the sadness in her voice, her eyes which had lost their lustre, her youthfulness which was wasting away waiting for a man who was long gone. This was the ultimate betrayal. A certain kind of cold callosity. Violence of a certain kind. Yet Nda still held hope that this man would someday come back. This was wishful thinking in my estimation but who am I to shake her out of her illusions? Things change all the time, though I am not sure of this. If he did not come back at the death of Eka, then this chapter might as well have been closed. This is why I approach marriage with trepidation and suspicion. No one should go through deceit of any kind. No one should go through this kind of violence. Not anyone, certainly not Nda.

My eyes travelled to her fingers as she spoke and rested on her wedding band. Nda never took it off. She always behaved like she still lived with her husband. I wondered who in their right senses would hurt a woman like this. I heard her call my name and realised I had wandered far in my thoughts.

"Are you still here?" she asked. I nodded, almost close to tears.

"You see, my life is mine, my sister. Yours need not stop because of your observations of people's actions and attitudes whilst married, including the observations of me and my life. There could be cautionary tales in this but don't stop your life.

I'm still wondering why you did not allow a date with Onyeka?" she asked, looking straight at me trying to elicit a response.

I remember the day she came to see me at my office during lunch with a man in tow. With twinkles in her eyes. I knew why the man was there. Nda has been on a mission to get me hitched, whilst on my part I continued to dodge a bullet. One look at the man and I could place his age at late thirties, early forties. He had a very strong build, was relatively tall and dark-skinned.

His mannerism was surprisingly gentle and softly spoken. After the exchange of pleasantries and introductions, I found out he had relocated back to the country and set up some kind of private business in construction. At the end of the visit, he asked for a date. I told him I would think about it and get back through Nda.

He laughed then and asked if Nda was going to be the go-between for two adults.

I told him yes.

It was a good visit. He seemed nice, warm and sincere. Yet

there seemed to be some kind of unreadiness and restraint on my own part to even begin to loosen up and give myself. Not yet! I agreed with myself. I should not create sadness for another person. So to Nda's question there's still no answer. The road to self-discovery and mastery is an intense one, often fraught with confusion and consternation of what could be.

I do not intend to get into a commitment of any sort without the mastery of myself. There must be that self-confidence and self-acceptance first before I give myself to another. I have to have the grit to go through the painful periods, the strange periods and the periods of unravelling.

The joy periods are always the first line of presentation. They have the ability to mask the real deal in marriage. The challenge often times is how do I appear and what attitudes do I display when I appear to the world or when people make demands of me? What parts should I play and how truthfully should I play them? How honest can I be in the commitment of myself to another? What will be my vulnerability ratio and what part of me will unravel as I open up my parts consistently in the contract of marriage?

Amadio, it is such a pity that you equally called at such a time as this to remind me of marriage.

I asked you what kind of marriage you expect of me; is it the type contracted on behalf of my country? The confluence of the Niger without their contributions and agreement to the nature of their pact? You laughed then and asked that I take a step forward. Any step forward would be just ok, you said. The marriage of my country and the way it was contracted keeps me awake at night. I told you that this one marriage that

I have experienced is just enough. I have not recovered from the bruises, the heartbreaks and the surprises it springs on me daily. Yet you brushed it aside, Amadio, and accused me of making excuses.

I sit here and laugh mirthlessly like a woman without teeth. Like an old woman with a mouth filled with red gums. My memories of yesterday are like an open sore yet I'm not satiated, neither am I assuaged. I should never take a step without checking and counting the cost. Any step whatsoever worth taking should be properly pondered on and analysed because you can either jump and sink or jump and scale. You urged me to jump regardless because it is not good for a woman to be alone. I think it takes a lot of courage, enormous courage, to live life, but it takes daunting, mountainous courage, grit and a lot of daring to be a woman and live as a woman.

Amadio! My life is passing through phases mired in changes. As my life takes shape I wonder at humans and life in general. I'm shocked at how people find time to determine who others are. I'm fascinated by how others judge others. I'm intrigued by how we smear mud on others and how we can malign people and tell strong lies against others simply by just knowing their names. The world is such a place. A daunting place filled with sorrowful and challenging narratives. Filled with people hungry for sad news and sad eulogies. I'm awakened by the urge of silence and what can happen when I decide to keep my silly judgments and opinions to myself, especially when I do not know all the facts or when the story is known to that person alone, or strange to me. There is a depth to a person which is understood by that person alone. Not even blood ties can fully reveal a person in their entirety. There's always a remaining mystery in every life, known and challenged by that person alone. It's even possible for someone not to have a full understanding of themselves.

We are first spiritual beings before we are physical, for who can explain fully the process of being a human right from the womb? No one can. I think it's an unfathomable, mysterious exchange. I always will stand askance in the face of a strange story. I will often think that however familiar a story is, I should be bold enough and courageous enough to accept that I may not understand its context or all of its elements. I should be truthful enough to avoid judging a story I do not understand. Its echoes may be familiar but its context and all its elements may be lost on me. It would then be a display of common sense to leave it alone or seek to understand it before releasing a volley of opinions that may be unwholesomely biased or prejudiced.

What happens to you when you are faced with the person you have become, the example you are becoming or have become? What happens to you?

What happens to you on the day you are opportune to meet yourself, know yourself and have the decency to understand yourself?

A man and himself can never merge unless in the humility of knowing of the essence of that man, the gradual discovery of purpose, the conceding of not knowing everything and the openness to new things and strange leanings. The acceptance of that man of how empty some of life's journey can become.

What is it that makes you want to stand in the place of surprise and confront yourself? What is it that helps you understand your soul as it brings you to that place of solemnity where he wants you to have that conversation with yourself? There are times when your spirit is deep and times when it is shallow. What is that thing that drives you to remove the laser on the layers of your defence when you face your spirit and your soul in truth? Are there times that you are done with life and all its throws at you? Are there times you welcome its crookedness with open hands and salute? How about the journey to its pain and its deep transformations? I ponder.

So now I'm done, fully done, even when I became totally undone as a woman. The moment I found clarity in this, my journey, Amadio, I embraced it with both hands. I welcomed it with my entire being. I have found purpose. I stood at the side of my house; it is actually my room but now it is empty. My bags are packed and tomorrow I begin my journey back to Awka where I have decided to take up a position as a teacher. The town of Awka awaits me and I am going back to the university, my alma mater. I have missed the classroom and I smell the chalk even now. Amadio, Nda said I was mad yesterday as I stayed up with her at her house for her final blessings and ablutions. I have stayed in Lagos for twelve years and I have had enough of both the bank job and the city for now. My soul yearns earnestly for the classroom for the diversity it can bring and the interactions that I hope to enjoy with the students.

Nda still thinks I am crazy and begged me to stay. Marriage still crept into our conversations late last night and she still asked that I get married before taking up the new job. And when I asked her what would happen if I did not consent to her request, the answer she gave me threw me off balance.

"Well, I've called Onyeka to take you to the park," she said and kept a straight face.

I started laughing and shook my head.

"Wow!" I said. "I hope you didn't, for your own sake, Nda!"

"Well, I did," she replied and still kept a straight face. "Come and beat me," she said in that Nigerian way, and with that, she started humming.

"You cannot be serious, Nda — without my permission?" I protested.

"Since you are very stubborn, there are many ways to kill a rat," she replied.

"But since the last time we spoke, I've not spoken to him again," I said.

"Because you blocked all the access to yourself, Ifedi. Don't I know you?" she said, almost shouting.

"I thought he travelled out of Lagos?" I asked.

"Yes, but he is back and he will take you to the park, Ifedi." She continued to tease me. "So get ready and do not sneak away before he comes, 'Nwa teacher'," she hailed me. We both burst into laughter. This, my teaching job, was a wonder to her. She refused to accept it.

"How can someone leave a corporate job for a teaching job in this economy?" she kept asking in disbelief, "Unless the person is as mad as Ifedinma Obiakor?"

"But then that's what my chi has agreed to, on my behalf," I retorted.

"Onye kwe chi ya ekwe literally means 'when one agrees, his or her personal god will agree also'," I said to her.

"No! That's what you choose for yourself, Ifedinma! Don't go calling your chi." I laughed then and she eyed me and hissed.

"Nda," I said calmly, "just allow me to go. I know you don't want to, but this is not goodbye. This is me trying to reclaim my life. It's hard, I know. But this is the only thing that can allow me the freedom to live my life in full and sanely."

"I know I cannot convince you," she said quietly. "I know that this makes you happy, but there is so much uncertainty in this country. Economically, this does not make sense," she said in an emotion-laden voice.

"I know what you're thinking, Nda, I hear the concern in your voice for me. But life should be lived bravely and life is actually filled with choices and I have chosen this. You know, at some point we either choose to live ultimately under the weather or to triumph over our challenges and take up our lives. And who knows what really makes economic sense? Who?" I asked. She looked up then and looked at me and smiled, her eyes glistening with tears.

"Thank you for all the times you were here giving me strength. Those students will be lucky to have you. May your road be rough," she said. When I heard what she said, my eyes flew up in surprise. There was silence for a bit. I shrugged.

"I understand," I finally said. She nodded and continued.

"The road will obey you as you journey. You will arrive in one piece." Amen! I said to her prayers and left.

We always pray this prayer for the road. We pray that the road will not be testy and neither should it consume us, the road users. Our roads are gulags, sadly. That's why we offer prayers any time we journey on their windy and snaky paths. There were tears on both sides, so I left immediately because I did not want her tears to keep me back. My mind was made up and my soul was also made up. There was no time to waste.

I am eternally grateful for the gift of this precious friendship, very rare in its form, so precious in its unravelling. I take it with me as I journey, often referencing it and drawing comfort from its depth. Not knowing if I will encounter it again, I relish it in all its entirety in a world that has become absolutely selfish in its nature as it ages.

The war within oneself never ends. The battle of this life is always changing its face and its bearing. Yet we continue to trudge on. My soul called me to return home to where I belong and that is simply what I have decided to do. I stand at the aspects of my life and I welcome the changes emptying themselves within me. I will never live in denial nor will I become an enemy to myself.

My life is wrapped up in the choices that I make. This one choice to get into my purpose to take up the chalk and try to change the narratives was most welcome, bearing in mind that this was a journey of self-discovery. I had to discover myself first before I could give of myself. I took one last look at the house that had held me and my worldly possessions for the last twelve years and some months and I bid it a warm farewell. Life was waiting for me and the journey would be endless.

As I stepped into the wee hours of the morning, it began to rain. I wondered what Nda was up to. She said she would not see me to the bus park. She cried so much on the last night and told me how she hates goodbyes, but life must continue, Amadio! The world is such a place, an intriguing place. I exhaled as the early morning dew hit my nostrils and I felt exhilarated. I carried with me a kind of story, a different kind of unravelling, and huge memories of the changes I had undergone.

As I heaved my luggage along, I hailed to the yellow and black taxis emerging from the hazy darkness translating into morning. I could barely make them out, it was so early. I felt a little heady, a little nostalgic, but with some kind of clarity and a bit of unsettling, which was strange. The morning had begun to open its bud and I could see its light lines on the horizon. I was thankful, so thankful to still be here in this country with its chameleonic nature, its never-ending challenges and struggles. And this journey, even though strangely familiar, was also an arduous task. I'm still lost in translation and wonder. Amadio, my joy is still in the hope that maybe, just maybe, one day our land will rejoice again and our hope will be renewed once more. I heard the sound of the Eastern buses as I alighted from the taxi and quicken my steps.

EPILOGUE

This is a cry,
a cry for the unknown country,
riddled with bullets of war yet snoring away.
Nothing left here,
barnyards are empty,
homes filled with cobwebs of sorrow,
emptiness of the echoes of its defeat,
heard in towns and villages.
Nothing left.

No spoils of war.
No victor, no vanquished.
They said then
the yesterday they refused to address
is in bed with them today, glaringly so.
Now it has taken a magical turn,
a satire in appearance and form, a dirge in approach
a kind of irony of vengeance;it has come home to roost.

The streets are empty.
Go home, they said.
Don't wait around.
The house that lies built is in crumbles,
its pangs of shame are heard amongst the nations.

As brilliant as it is together with its people
it cannot realise its potential, neither can it save itself.

Go home,
they say,
even as they have
their hands in the communal till
with sweat oozing from their pores.
Yet shame is very alien to them.
I kind of hear the sounds of yesterday.
Artilleries moved in on a people
with children of sunken eyes,
women of bare breasts
denied of their husbands,
their children fodder to the barrels of guns,
soup pots of cassava leaves.

Yesterday is fast upon us
yet we cannot see.
This is an epitaph of a certain kind,
an ode to evildoers,
a dirge to a country.
The evening of our lives is here.
How do we find the pathways to home
as the twilight takes its branches?
Who will light our paths again
and oil our brains?
For now, the centre can no longer hold.

Things have indeed fallen apart.

The die is cast,

the birds are home to roost. These are birds of a certain nature.

They find solace in the macabre,

they love the repulsive and the rotten,

they grovel in the deluge of rotten carcasses.

Birds of a nature.

Vultures of a certain kind.

CPSIA information can be obtained
at www.ICGtesting.com
Printed in the USA
LVHW100712140322
713251LV00037B/2107

9 781914 560286